*Look what people are saying
about these talented authors!*

Of Tori Carrington...

"Get out the asbestos gloves to read this one,
it's almost too hot to handle."
—*Writers Unlimited* on *Reckless*

"Consistently excellent authors
with surprising emotional depth."
—*The Romance Readers Connection* on *Reckless*

"One of category's most talented authors."
—*EscapetoRomance.com*

Of Kate Hoffmann...

"Sexy and wildly romantic."
—*RT Book Reviews* on *Doing Ireland*

"Fully developed characters and perfect pacing
make this story feel completely right."
—*RT Book Reviews* on *Your Bed or Mine*

"Sexy, heartwarming and romantic...
a story to settle down with and enjoy—
and then re-read."
—*RT Book Reviews* on *The Mighty Quinns: Teague*

ABOUT THE AUTHORS

RT Book Reviews Career Achievement Award–winning, bestselling duo Lori Schlachter Karayianni and Tony Karayianni are the power behind the pen name **Tori Carrington.** Their more than fifty novels include numerous Blaze miniseries, as well as the ongoing Sofie Metropolis, P.I. comedic mystery series with another publisher. Visit www.toricarrington.net and www.sofiemetro.com for more information.

Kate Hoffmann began writing for Harlequin Books in 1993. Since then she's published nearly seventy books, primarily in the Temptation and Blaze lines. When she isn't writing, she enjoys music, theatre and musical theatre. She is active working with high school students in the performing arts. She lives in southeastern Wisconsin with her cat, Chloe.

Tori Carrington
Kate Hoffmann

BLAZING BEDTIME STORIES:
VOLUME VI

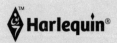

™
Harlequin®

TORONTO NEW YORK LONDON
AMSTERDAM PARIS SYDNEY HAMBURG
STOCKHOLM ATHENS TOKYO MILAN MADRID
PRAGUE WARSAW BUDAPEST AUCKLAND

ISBN-13: 978-0-373-79679-3

BLAZING BEDTIME STORIES, VOLUME VI

Copyright © 2012 by Harlequin Books S.A.

The publisher acknowledges the copyright holders
of the individual works as follows:

MAID FOR HIM...
Copyright © 2012 by Lori Karayianni and Tony Karayianni

OFF THE BEATEN PATH
Copyright © 2012 by Peggy A. Hoffmann

Recycling programs
for this product may
not exist in your area.

www.Harlequin.com

Printed in U.S.A.

CONTENTS

TORI CARRINGTON

Maid for Him...

This book is dedicated to blazing fairy tale
lovers everywhere. And to Brenda Chin,
for being an awesome editor and
an even more awesome human being.

1

WILD WIND BLOWING, water swirling, pressure building, an untamed torrent assaulting from without and filling the blood within.

Daphne Moore found something fundamentally intoxicating about nature's violent tempests; storms had a way of clearing away toxic debris, cleansing the soul, baring what was important.

And they served as a reminder of why she'd chosen the sea over land nearly ten years ago, why she would permanently confirm that decision in one short week.

Beneath the churning surface of the Pacific Ocean off the coast of Southern California, the sea was calm… still…beautiful.

Leisurely swishing the fish tail that was her body from the waist down forth and back, she glided through the welcoming water, relishing the feel of it against the upper part of her body that was still human, her breasts tingling, her long red hair flowing back from her face as she went.

Land or sea?

When she was presented the choice on the day of her sixteenth birthday by her parents, she hadn't hesitated: the sea. It was here that she belonged; here that she was needed.

The chaos of man interested her not at all.

She eased to a stop, keeping herself stationary with a barely noticeable wave of her long, silvery green tail, watching a school of tuna swim by, a spectacle of movement and glinting silver, the storm raging above having little to do with their forever restless movements.

She smiled and reached out to skim her fingers against the smooth flesh of one of the dolphins that inevitably followed the tuna, on the lookout for the sharks that trailed them.

Down here, everything made sense. There was a natural order she found predictable, comforting.

Including mermaid rules.

At sixteen, a choice was extended to both children born of committed mermaids and those born of those who had chosen the human route: join us. Live life as a merperson or as a human. It was more of a ritual decision, since the ability to take either form remained.

Until you were twenty-five and asked to make a final choice.

Her mother had chosen life as a human.

Daphne intended to choose life as a mermaid.

The tuna and dolphins moved on, leaving her momentarily alone.

If every now and again she experienced loneliness…well, that was between her and the coral reef deep below. She understood it had nothing to do with her love of the sea.

Rather it was love, itself, that posed the problem. Both of the familial and romantic variety.

Sure, there were negative aspects connected to her decision, as there were with any choice. First and foremost, she didn't see her land-loving parents as much as she would have liked. Outside of her not-so-frequent land visits, and their occasional outings to see her on their sailing runs, she rarely saw them. And until they invented a cell phone that operated on something other than electricity…well, she couldn't exactly call them at will.

The other…?

Well, there weren't very many of her kind making the same decision she had. Her breed was fast approaching extinction, the lure and luxuries of man proving too great a temptation to most at the tender age of sixteen, when all were asked to choose.

Which meant potential mates were sadly lacking.

And undoubtedly, her restlessness had a lot to do with her recent infatuation with a man who coasted on top of her beloved sea, but never ventured into it…

Daphne looked up toward the shifting surface, at the all too familiar hull of the sailboat some fifty yards to the west, the nearby anchor too far from the bottom to be effective against the storm's violent intentions.

His name was Kieran Morrison, his fifty-foot classic schooner was named *Come Sail Away,* and he fascinated her unlike any other human male before him.

Swishing her powerful tail, she swam upward, breaking through the surface just as lightning brightened the storm-darkened, early morning sky, bringing everything into electric blue relief. She immediately spotted Kieran, struggling with one of the sails that had lashed loose in the wind, his white T-shirt melded to his powerful torso, his jeans soaked to the core, his dark hair plastered to his forehead, his features pulled into a determined grimace.

So handsome…

So sexy…

So forbidden…

He'd never seen her. And he never would. Her interest in him would have to remain one-sided. No matter how strongly she was drawn to him and the shadows that clung to him like his now wet clothes. No matter how much she wanted to smooth back his hair and kiss the deep, sad frown from his lips. No matter how much she longed to feel his magnificent hands on her skin and scales.

Another bolt of lightning lit the sky and she found herself staring straight into his midnight-black eyes.

Daphne went still.

The first rule in merpeople relations was that there were no mermaid relations. In order to remain separate and protected, man must never know of their existence. They could never be anything more than a legend told by old sea captains or else suffer the consequences, which included relentless hunting by unique prey-seeking predators far more dangerous than any great white.

Yet in that one moment, Daphne found herself unable to break free from his gaze, every part of her tingling to brilliant, exciting life…

HE WAS SPENDING too much time at sea….

Kieran Morrison knew a moment of gravity as he stood staring out into the waves, sure he'd seen a woman bobbing out there in the thrashing water, looking calm in the midst of the storm.

But that was impossible. The marina manager had warned him not to go out, that to do so would be suicidal, so he hadn't expected anyone else to be out. And he'd seen no other boats. If she'd been tossed from a craft, surely she'd be signaling for help.

His schooner listed dangerously, forcing him to grab the main mast to steady himself. When he looked back out, the vision was gone.

And she had been a vision. All long red hair, huge green eyes, iridescent skin and high, stiff-tipped breasts that teased the water's surface.

Damn, he was losing it.

Of course, if you listened to his mother, he'd lost it long ago. Certainly before he'd married Clarissa Miles five years ago, although much less after their nasty divorce six months ago.

He dragged his hand across his wet hair and wiped the mixture of salt and rain water from his eyes. He was seeing things. It was as simple as that. There had been no woman bobbing in those waves looking at him with large, soulful eyes. He'd merely imagined her. She'd been nothing more than a fantasy conjured up from his sex-starved mind. Something his subconscious mind had created to give him an option more enticing than any he'd find on shore. An escape from money-hungry exes, over-worrying parents, demanding business partners and ceaselessly matchmaking friends.

The sailboat listed again, nearly tossing him overboard.

He, on the other, was very real, indeed. And although he may have vaguely wished for his end over the past few months, ever since he'd traded his hectic life at the successful commercial fishing venture he owned in partnership with his best friend Mike Dunlop for the tranquility of the sea itself, this wasn't exactly how he'd envisioned it.

Trying to steady the runaway boom, he was afraid his realization had come too late...

Damn it all to hell. Was he doomed to run into every wall life had to offer? He'd wanted nothing more than to...

To...

His mind went blank.

That had been the way of things lately. He wasn't sure what he wanted anymore. He only knew that the only thing that brought him peace anymore was being out on his sailboat. And he was lucky to have worked hard over the past decade and was wealthy enough to afford to sail as little or as often as he liked.

As far as women went…

Well, they weren't even a part of the landscape. Not after his last experience.

Why, then, was he imagining beautiful women bobbing in the stormy sea?

No, not women—a woman.

A singularly phenomenal one who'd been looking back at him as intensely as he'd been looking at her.

Mike was right. He needed to get laid.

Problem was, he couldn't bring himself to talk to a woman long enough to get her number, much less get her back to his place.

He really needed to get his shit together.

The wind and rain whipped at him at once as if in agreement…reminding him that he had more pressing matters to concern himself with at the moment.

The boom swung out of his grip. His bare feet slid on the deck as the sailboat listed toward starboard. He scrambled to grab on to the mast but it was just beyond his reach. He looked wildly around for something, *anything* to stop him from going overboard…only to find the boom swinging back in his direction. He lifted his hands to stop it. Too late. It hit him clean in the head.

The last thing he saw was water—lots of it—before sinking below the surface of the sea…

SHE SHOULDN'T BE here…shouldn't be doing this. But oh, how nice it was to see him up close and personal.

Daphne lay against the teak deck of the sailboat, knowing enough about the human world and its material possessions to understand the worth of the schooner, as well as the owner's attention to detail and care of his possession.

She knew about the human world because she'd lived the majority of her first sixteen years in human form. She hadn't known she'd had a choice...until her mother had sat her down and told her otherwise.

She'd eagerly chosen the sea over continued life as the only child of a wealthy Southern Californian couple whom she loved madly, but had no desire to emulate. While her one-time mermaid mother had tried to mask her sadness at her only child's decision, she hadn't succeeded. But she had supported it.

Or, rather, she'd supported Daphne.

Now, however, it wasn't the sailboat that captured Daphne's attention, but its striking owner, who now slept easily in the warm sunshine.

She knew she should slip back into the water, that she should have the moment she realized he would be okay after the boom knocked him flat out and into the water. She'd swum after him, brought him to the surface and managed with tremendous effort, to get his lifeless body back up on deck where she'd monitored him until she'd judged his vitals to be within normal range. But she needed to regain her physical and emotional bearings. And surely there was nothing wrong with watching him as he slept off the remnants of his ordeal?

She'd nursed various sea creatures back to health over the years—nudging those beyond her expertise toward the beach and care beyond her ability to provide—so it was difficult to convince herself she was staying to make sure he would be all right. The storm had passed, the waters had calmed, and now she lay next to him, measuring his size against her own, taking comfort in his even breathing, wading in the dangerous pool of need spreading throughout her for this man.

While it was easy to dismiss her attraction to him as lack of options, well, that didn't hold any sway now. Not when she was so close she could smell him…kiss him…

Over a month had passed since she first spotted him out on his sailboat alone. He'd been squinting dark eyes into the sunset, although she'd doubted he'd seen a single ray. It wasn't hard to see that his thoughts had been turned inward.

Nearly every day afterward, she'd seen him again, following when he veered in different directions, secretly hoping he might see her, sense her presence like a soft whisper.

Then five days ago, he'd disappeared…

With the lightest of touches, she traced her fingertip along the line of his nose, down over his lips and along his strong jaw. She'd been afraid that whatever had driven him to the sea had righted itself, taking him away from her.

Then, yesterday, he'd returned in the midst of the storm, looking as lost as ever.

Daphne lay her head against her outstretched arm, basking in the warmth of the sun and her desire for him. How she'd love to feel him, inside and out.

She shivered, her lips tingling, her nipples hardening and her fin stiffening.

To make love to him...

Her eyes began drifting closed. A quiet alarm bell sounded somewhere in the back of her mind, but she was too intoxicated with wanting him to pay it much heed. Instead, she sighed softly and drifted off to the only place where she was free to be with the only man she'd ever wanted....

GARDENIAS...

The exotic scent filled Kieran's senses as he stirred from sleep. A dull ache at the back of his head drew his hand there. For a moment, he was afraid he was in New Orleans after a particularly nasty three-day bender. Then he remembered the storm, the swinging boom and the consuming waves of the sea...

He cracked open his eyes, wincing against the bright sunlight, surprised to find himself on the deck of his sailboat. Hadn't he fallen overboard?

He absently rubbed his face, trying to make sense out of the situation.

Well, at least the storm had passed. And judging by the gentle lapping of the Pacific against the hull, the sea had calmed. He raised to his elbows to take in the damage...and his gaze fell on the sleeping figure next to him.

It was the woman from last night.

The one bobbing in the water.

The vision he'd been sure he'd imagined…

He blinked.

Then blinked again.

Her red hair glimmered in the sun and her skin was whiter than bleached driftwood. The tips of her breasts were rosy and taut, her waist impossibly slender.

But it wasn't any of those facts that surprised him; he already knew she was beautiful.

But the six-foot tail and fin where her legs and feet should be definitely made him question his sanity.

Holy shit…

He struggled to sit, to get a closer look, to touch the fascinating creature to confirm she actually did exist.

Was it him or was she glistening? As if a soft mist clung to her skin and scales?

His gaze fastened on the shadows of her lashes against her cheeks, the perfect line of her lips, the pearl that hung on a gold chain around her neck… He knew such an incredible desire to kiss her, he couldn't resist.

He slowly leaned in, the scent of gardenias once again surrounding him, telling him the fragrance was coming from her, was *her*. He wasn't sure what he expected when his lips brushed hers, but it certainly wasn't the rose petal softness, the searing heat, the arc of instant connection which sparked in him an urgent need for more…

She made a soft sound and he watched as her lashes

fluttered, then her eyes opened, revealing the most electric pair of green eyes he'd ever gazed into.

In them, he saw first surprise, then sweet surrender....

And then she kissed him back.

Kieran groaned in the back of his throat, his arousal so complete, his entire body throbbed along with his hard erection.

He skimmed his fingertips down, grazing them over her nipple.

The loud honking of a watercraft horn rent the air in two.

No...

He reluctantly pulled away, turning completely in order to see the coast-guard cutter in the distance.

He got to his feet to wave that he—they—were okay as the cutter quickly closed the hundred-yard gap between their boats. He wished they'd quickly go away so he could further explore the almost...magical sensations he was experiencing.

He turned to look at her...

Only to find her gone.

Kieran rushed to the side of the boat, shielding his eyes from the sunlight as he searched for some sign of her in the water. He saw nothing.

Damn...

It wasn't possible he'd imagined her twice in as many hours...

Was it?

He turned back, taking in the residual dampness on

the deck where she'd been lying next to him. The glint of something white drew his eye. He bent over to finger the object before picking it up.

A pearl. One perfectly shaped, natural pearl nearly as large as a quarter, bigger than any he'd ever seen.

He looked out at the sea again. He swore he saw something shifting just beneath the surface. He looked harder, only to watch as fish swam by in a swiftly, glistening school.

He wasn't imaging things.

Damn it all to hell, please tell him he wasn't imaging things.

His life had been so devoid of emotion, of meaning, of focus for so long now, he'd forgotten what it felt like, what it meant to want something.

And he wanted her....

2

"Let me get this straight… You saw a mermaid."

Kieran frowned at his old friend and longtime business partner Mike Dunlop. "Yes. No."

He waved for the bartender at the San Clemente hotel, near the joint commercial fishing venture main offices of Morrison and Dunlop, Limited, to give him another double of bourbon. A day had passed since he'd awakened on the deck of the schooner next to the gorgeous, slumbering redhead. And he'd spent a great chunk of the time since then, trying to find out who she was, where she belonged or if anyone else had spotted her.

When his houseman Samuel had called with the reminder of the drinks meeting with Mike, it had been too late to cancel, or else he would have.

Hiring Samuel to look after things for him home side was one of the smartest decisions Kieran had ever made. He'd done it primarily so the house wouldn't be left empty for long stretches, but Samuel did far more than collect the mail and newspapers. He'd come to be Kieran's personal assistant, butler, manager and friend.

"I already thought you were spending too much time on that damn boat," Mike said. "Now I'm convinced you're suffering sunstroke."

Funny, that's what the coast-guard guys had said, too. Or, rather, that he might be suffering from exposure. They'd recommended he check into a nearby hospital for observation.

"I didn't just see her," Kieran stressed, all too aware he was treading water much more dangerous than the stormy sea he'd been in the other day. "She was sleeping next to me."

"Uh-huh." Mike shook his head at the tender as he started to pour Kieran a second bourbon. "I think my friend here has had enough."

Kieran motioned for the tender to continue. "You were the only one who believed my story about finding Catwoman outside my bedroom window."

"We were ten. And I wanted to believe you. Moreover, I was hoping to see her outside mine."

Kieran swirled the amber liquid in his glass but didn't take a sip. Maybe everyone was right. Maybe he was suffering from exposure to the elements.

The only problem with that? The pearl he carried around in his pocket, the one he was hesitant to show anyone. He wasn't sure why. Didn't it serve as physical proof that he'd seen her?

Then why not share it?

He found himself holding the item in question inside

his pocket, feeling it warm beneath his touch, imagining the smoothness of her skin, the heat of her kiss.

He forced himself to let go of the pearl.

"And you say she rescued you? Are you sure she didn't make you run aground?"

"You're thinking of a Siren."

"Oh, yeah."

Kieran and Mike went back a long ways. Back to England where Mike's American family had moved into the flat next to Kieran's. His father had been an attaché with the American Embassy and despite their differences, the two boys had formed a fast and hard bond. They'd become so close that when Mike's family had moved back to the States when he was a teen, Kieran had gone with them, completing his junior year in high school with him in California, then college.

It was only natural they'd go into business together, starting their joint commercial fishing venture that had been turning a healthy profit for years.

Unfortunately, when things turned south personally for Kieran, his friend had been at a loss as what to do.

Mostly because Kieran didn't have a clue about what *he* wanted to do.

Until now...

"Well, got to tell you, pal, that's some fish tale," Mike said. "Gives new meaning to the saying, 'I caught one *this* big.'" He stretched out his arms to indicate the length of the fish.

Kieran smiled and shook his head.

"So," Mike said. "You ready to come back to work yet?"

It had been three months since Kieran had stepped foot inside Morrison and Dunlop. Funny, when they'd started the venture ten years ago, he'd somehow thought he'd be spending time at sea. Instead, he'd seen more of the inside of his office that overlooked the waters he'd much rather be out on.

So when he'd woken up nearly six months ago to find his faithless wife had left him for a business associate, divorce papers on the pillow next to him—papers in which she claimed half of everything for which he'd worked so hard and sacrificed so much—well, he'd thought it was long past time to make a few corrections.

"I still think you should have fought her," Mike said, as if reading his thoughts.

Kieran downed the bourbon and stretched his neck. "We're in California, remember?"

"Yes, but you began the company before you even met her."

"True."

What was also true was that he'd wanted the divorce over as quickly as possible. So he'd had his own attorney draw up a couple of amendments and within a week, it was a done deal.

And in the five days, which followed the final decree, the waiting period would be over and he'd be officially divorced.

At his signal the bartender poured him another and he sipped it, denying himself the urge to down it.

"I somehow never saw myself being divorced."

"I never saw you being married."

Kieran chuckled. "Yeah."

His friend had a point there. For the most part, he'd enjoyed being a bachelor, calling his own shots, dating when convenient. Then he'd met Clarissa six years ago and begun walking down the road he guessed every guy walked sooner or later. They'd dated, moved in together, then married.

"At least you didn't have kids."

If his friend had said that even a month ago, Kieran might have agreed. Now, well, now he couldn't help wondering if children might have saved their marriage.

The memory of the sexy redhead slinked into his mind…

"You know, the company needs you," Mike said, moving his own empty glass of beer toward the tender. "You've been away too long."

He took him in. "No…and yeah."

The company didn't need him. At this point, it ran pretty much like a well-oiled machine, mechanisms in place that meant he didn't have to be there like he once had. Hell, for the past couple of years, he'd been little more than an annoying supervisor, keeping on top of those already competently doing their jobs.

He told Mike as much, but his friend disagreed.

"Have you taken a look at the semiannual reports?" he asked.

"No. Why? Should I have?"

His friend stared at him.

He chuckled. "Come on. Not that much could have changed in three months."

Mike drank from his replenished glass as Kieran's cell phone rang.

"Sorry. I thought I turned it off." He fished it out of his pocket and looked at the display. His mother.

Damn.

"Hold on. I've got to take this."

He slid from the stool and walked toward the door of the upscale restaurant.

"Hello, darling," Liz Morrison said in her pitch-perfect British accent.

"Hello, Mum. How are you?" Since he'd now lived as much in the States as he had in the U.K., his accent was more American, but it always seemed to favor his parents' whenever he spoke or spent time with them. Which hadn't been often lately.

"I'm fine. Ready for our trip. The car is set to ring around in a few short hours. We're looking forward to seeing you and Clarissa. It's been much too long."

Kieran stopped walking, nearly causing the man behind him to plow into him.

Oh, hell. He'd completely forgotten his parents were coming for a visit.

He ran his free hand through his hair several times. It was too late to make excuses; they would be on a plane in a matter of hours.

He briefly closed his eyes. Boy, were they ever going to be surprised to find out that not only were they not likely to have a grandchild anytime soon, but he was no longer with the one woman who might have given them one.

He squinted as he thought about the redhead...

"Not encouraging," his mother said. "Your silence, that is."

"What? Oh, sorry, Mum. I was just a little distracted, that's all."

"So you do look forward to seeing us then."

"Of course, I look forward to seeing you. In fact, I'm planning to pick you up at the airport."

"Good then."

They spoke for a couple of minutes more about itineraries and his father and then he wished her a safe trip and hung up, standing stone still holding his cell phone as if it were a grenade, afraid that if he released it, it would explode.

What was he talking about? His life already resembled a war zone.

And the redhead stood as the sole spot of color amongst the ashes.

"Hey," Mike said, coming outside to join him.

Kieran stared at where he still held the phone and then put it in his pocket, feeling the pearl again as he did so.

"I'm going to have to head out. You may no longer have a wife, but mine just texted me that dinner's getting cold. That's code for get home now."

Kieran chuckled and gave him a bro hug. "Good seeing you."

"Would be better to see more of you. Like at the office."

"Pass."

"Look at those reports."

"I will."

They parted company and Kieran walked to his car, making a mental list of all he had to do between now and his parents' arrival.

And wanting to do nothing but drive to Dana Point Marina and get on his boat to go in search of the woman he couldn't seem to dislodge from his mind....

3

DAPHNE SMOOTHED HER hands down over her hips, tendrils of awareness rippling over her human skin. This quite possibly might be the last time she traded her tail for legs and slipped into a slinky, designer evening gown for one of her parents' charitable events. Tonight's gala was in honor of keeping the oceans clean.

Or, rather, in honor of the seas she and her mother loved. While her human father could respect the waters from which they'd come, he could never understand the depth of their emotion.

Daphne also suspected her mother had chosen her favorite charity, and this particular time before her daughter's ultimate dedication as a mermaid, in Daphne's honor.

For the first time, she experienced what she could only guess was a pang of sadness.

Up until now, joy and conviction had ruled her emotions.

Was it perhaps because of the finality of her decision? The limitations her confirmation would put on her life from here on out? The natural distance she would place forever between her and her parents?

Or could it be connected to the man to whom she had unintentionally revealed herself?

Her fingers fluttered to her throat where the pearl she'd been given when she was sixteen usually lay. The same pearl she'd left behind on Kieran's sailboat.

She felt bare without it.

Yet strangely…liberated.

She told herself she'd left it behind accidentally. Because to consider otherwise…

She caught her dreamy-eyed expression in the mirror.

The pearl, which was given at a mermaid's sixteenth birthday ceremony represented reaching adulthood and was to be kept in the recipient's possession at all times. Until…

Daphne swallowed hard.

Until that mermaid chose her mate for life…

"Your gown fits like a glove," Cecelia Moore said from the doorway.

Daphne smiled at her mother in the mirror. "All things being equal, I prefer my fins."

She picked up a bottle of body oil from the dressing table in her old bedroom and smoothed a generous amount over her arms. She'd already oiled her legs twice and probably would again before going down to the party that was already in full swing downstairs in her parents' sweeping Newport Beach estate.

The charity was one she'd helped establish and benefited efforts to keep the seas clean and free.

After all, next week, the seas would be her home…

She considered the long, white gown that bore pearly sequins in an artsy design, from the single wide shoulder strap down diagonally across her body. Her mother had outdone herself in choosing her wardrobe tonight. But, of course, she always did.

Daphne sat down on an embroidered chair and swept aside the skirt, the sight of her long, lean legs increasingly seeming unfamiliar. She picked up the oil bottle.

"Are you all right?"

Cecelia came inside and stood behind the chair, resting a hand on the back while she searched Daphne's face in the mirror.

"Yes. Why?"

Her mother smiled softly. "You seem…a little distracted."

She supposed that was one way to refer to her emotional state.

She smoothed the oil along her skin. "Actually, I have a question for you."

"You know you can ask me anything."

Yes, her mother had always been generous that way. But in her desire to allow her only child to make her own decisions, there had been some topics that had been off-limits. Oh, not barred, just avoided.

This one in particular.

"Do you ever regret…well, you know." She met the

reflection of her mother's green gaze. "Do you ever regret giving up the sea for Dad?"

There had been only one other time that they'd discussed Cecelia being born to the sea. That she'd known only the sea…until she met Patrick Moore when they were teens during a chance surfing encounter.

"No."

The word was said so adamantly Daphne was forced to look away for fear of what her own gaze might reveal.

She felt her mother's hand on her shoulder. "Are you having second thoughts?"

Was she?

Ever since she was four and her parents had taken her on a beach vacation—one where her fins had first appeared during a prolonged swim in the water—she'd been drawn to the sea; she'd felt more at home there than anywhere else. She looked around her richly appointed bedroom that had always seemed to belong to someone else. As a child, she'd had an imaginary friend who always seemed more comfortable there. Her name had been Portia and she had always loved the opulence and parties.

It had helped Daphne participate with at least a modicum of acceptance, if not complete enjoyment.

It was only when she was swimming in the depths of the blue sea that she felt sheer bliss and delight.

"Who is he?"

Startled, Daphne nearly dropped the bottle.

She righted it, secured the cap then put it on the dressing table. "Who?"

"The man you're thinking about."

She laughed. "I'm not thinking about a man."

The word *thinking* seemed such an inadequate word. If she'd thought she was infatuated before kissing him, now...

Well, now she seemed to be in a constant state of awareness, her breasts tender, her female parts longing for something she hadn't known before.

Her mother's smile was knowing.

Daphne looked down and away, feeling her cheeks flush.

There was a brief knock at the door before her father opened it. "Decent?"

"Yes," they both answered.

He grinned, taking them both in. "I'd say that's arguable."

Daphne got up, smiling as she took his hands and kissed him warmly on both cheeks. If he held her a little too tightly, she pretended not to notice. Unlike her mother, he had never known the sea. And he was clearly puzzled and hurt by her decision to limit herself to it.

She drew back and smiled into his face. He was so handsome. So charming.

"You look lovely," he said, squeezing her hands before releasing them.

"Thanks."

Daphne stepped back and allowed him to embrace

her mother. As always, she felt as though she were intruding somehow and had to glance away. There was so much intimacy there it was difficult to witness without feeling like she was seeing something she shouldn't, although there was certainly nothing indecent about the exchange.

Just blindingly and honestly beautiful.

"Are we ready?" her father asked, tucking her mother's arm into the crook of his, then offering his other arm to her.

Daphne easily took it, wondering if any other man could wear a tuxedo as well.

Moments later, as they descended the curving, marble staircase to the ballroom-size foyer, and she immediately met the gaze of the man who had started a fateful ball rolling, she knew that there was...

KIERAN NEARLY CHOKED on his drink.

The last place he would have expected to see the knockout redhead was walking down the stairs of this house. Actually, the last place he would have expected to see her was walking down any stairs at all....

He absently wiped the back of his hand against his mouth as his gaze glided down her long, long legs to where very real feet were clad in very sexy sandals.

"Sir?"

A waiter was holding out a linen napkin to him. He accepted it, glancing down to where he'd spilled a bit of his drink on the front of his tux, then thanked the man, blotting at the dampness.

He'd be lucky if that's the only damage he walked away with tonight.

The waiter accepted the napkin and took his drink, promising to be back with another.

And to think, he'd nearly tossed the longstanding invitation to this charitable event away this morning when his house manager had placed it in his inbox. While keeping the naturalists pacified, if not happy, had been part of his job before, the only items on his agenda was preparing himself for his parents arrival in the morning…and continuing his search for the striking beauty he'd found on his boat, the one everyone was trying to tell him didn't exist outside his imagination.

Now here she was…

And she seemed as surprised to see him as he was to see her…

It took every ounce of self-control he had to stop himself from going straight to her, demanding to know who she was and what she had been doing on his boat… and swirling in his mind like a sexy fog, driving him to distraction.

Then again, he wasn't all that convinced he could have moved had he tried. His feet seemed to have sprouted roots, fixing him to the spot as surely as time-strengthened vines.

Who was she? It was safe to say she was connected in some way to their hosts, the Moores. He'd known Patrick Moore for years, through the charity he and his wife headed, which was what tonight's event was about.

But her…?

He watched as she greeted the line waiting at the bottom of the staircase along with the Moores, her rich hair catching the light, her smile flashing, her eyes seeking him out with every other word she spoke.

Was she remembering their kiss? Had she experienced the same white-hot flash of heat he had? Had she thought about him with a single-minded obsession since she disappeared from the deck of his sailboat?

The waiter brought him another drink. He took his hand from his pocket where he rolled the pearl between his finger and accepted it, only to place it on a nearby coaster on a table as he cut a path toward her.

He had to confirm she was real, that she wasn't another figment of his imagination.

He had to know if she was the one person who could save his life more than in a literal sense…

She gasped when he lightly touched her bare shoulder, turning toward him as one might a predator.

"I'm sorry," he said quietly. "I didn't mean to startle you…."

Though he'd withdrawn his hand, his fingers tingled from the brief contact, as if he'd come in contact with an electrical source. And her reaction told him she'd been just as affected by the contact, though his fingers had barely grazed her skin.

"Daphne?" asked the woman he guessed was Moore's wife, openly looking at him. "Everything all right?"

The redhead didn't appear to hear at first. He guessed she was just as incapable of speech as he was.

He saw so much there, in her eyes. Answers to questions he hadn't voiced. Questions to answers not yet given.

Desire, pure and powerful and all-consuming.

Finally, she said, "Yes, yes, Mother. Everything's... fine."

Kieran barely registered her name and the connection. He was mesmerized by the pink in her cheeks and the bowing of her lips.

"May I speak with you?" he asked.

He didn't miss her deep swallow as she considered his question.

"I'm sorry, do I know you?"

He felt the faintest tinge of amusement. She knew very well who he was. Just as he knew who she was, with or without fins.

"Oh, yes, I'd say you do." He took her hand in his, feeling that same electric shock. "But officially, my name is Kieran. Kieran Morrison." He covered her hand with his other. "And you're Daphne."

"Kieran," Patrick Moore said, spotting him. "I'm glad you could make it."

He was forced to release Daphne's hand in order to shake her father's.

"I see you've met my daughter," Patrick said. "And my wife—"

"I haven't had the honor," Daphne's mother said, standing on Daphne's other side as if protecting her. "Cecelia Moore."

"Kieran here owns Morrison and Dunlop."

"Co-owns," he corrected.

Daphne's brows rose as she absorbed the information. He gathered she didn't miss the irony of his being a fisherman. Or, rather, co-owner of a fishing company.

"Nice to finally meet you, Mrs. Moore—"

"Cecelia, please."

"Very well then, Cecelia. You won't mind if I borrow your daughter for just a moment, will you?"

Was it him, or did Cecelia look to Daphne as if for reassurance it was okay with her?

"If you'll excuse me," Patrick said. "I hear the orchestra has started, which means I'm expected to officially welcome everyone. Please, Kieran, make yourself at home."

"Thank you," he said, hoping it was loud enough to be heard, but feeling oddly like he'd whispered. The moment he spotted her on the steps, the world had begun slowly drifting away in a blinding white light, and she was the only spot of color.

"Dance with me?" he asked.

4

JUST ONCE…

She wanted to feel his touch just one time…

That was the solitary thought that flowed through Daphne's mind when she found herself at Kieran's San Clemente house an hour later, standing on his large, private balcony that boasted a spectacular, moonlit view of the Pacific in the distance, but was too far away to smell.

He, on the other hand, filled her senses more powerfully than the sea.

"God, you're so beautiful…."

The words might have sounded insincere coming from anyone else, but when combined with the urgency in his voice, and the restlessness of his touch, they ranked among the most honest she'd ever heard.

He made her feel beautiful. Something she'd never experienced.

She'd known this was where they'd end up the moment she'd agreed to dance with him. She'd known that once she felt his hand discreetly brush against her lower back, pressing her against him, that she'd want more.

She'd known when she'd opened her eyes to find him kissing her the morning before, she'd be unable to turn away from the connection that had formed between them in that instant...fused them together in a way she had yet to completely understand.

So when he'd whispered that he wanted to be alone with her, she hadn't hesitated.

There was no time for games. No need to worry about appearing loose or easy. This was about sheer surrender. A onetime thing she hoped to take with her after her final dedication to the sea, something to cherish to the end of her days.

He brushed his lips against her temple as soft jazz drifted through the open French doors. Her eyes drifted closed, and her pulse thrummed, immersing her fully in the moment.

She'd wanted him from afar for so long she'd never dared dream she'd be standing this close to him. And now that she was, she refused to succumb to doubt or worry.

She'd sensed his presence in her parents' foyer before visually spotting him. Just as she had always known when he had his schooner out. She felt...bound to him in a way she'd never experience with anyone else save her parents. And while she could, she intended to explore this connection as far as she dared.

"I'm so afraid that if I let go of you, you'll disappear again," he whispered into her hair.

She tilted her chin into her chest and smiled, then raised her head to stare into his dark eyes.

"I'm not going anywhere...."

"Promise?"

She nodded slightly. "Promise."

"Not even if I ask why you left me yesterday morning?"

It was a dream standing there, holding her in his arms, gently swaying to a song he couldn't really hear. Not that he needed to hear it. His heart beat a rhythm he couldn't help but move to.

Move closer to her...

He wasn't sure why he'd asked what he had. He told himself what had transpired yesterday would be better left unmentioned. But before he could stop himself, he was saying the words...and needing to hear the response.

Problem was, he was afraid he wasn't going to get one.

She held his gaze, her kissable lips tilted upward in a small smile, but she remained silent. He supposed he should be glad she wasn't denying the encounter. Or that she wasn't retracting her promise to stay.

God, was she truly there?

He inhaled, taking in the scent of gardenias and the sea. He wanted to kiss her so badly, he physically ached. But somehow, just knowing he would was enough for now. He held her, swayed with her, feeling need surge through his bloodstream like a strong drink.

If you'd have asked him a week ago what he'd be doing tonight, the last thing he would have said was entertaining a beautiful woman in his house. Especially after his divorce…

He closed his eyes and drew her closer. He wasn't going to think about that now, didn't want to taint such beauty with ugliness.

Besides, this…whatever it was…transcended all.

Within a blink of her lovely eyes, she'd brought a full color pallet to his drab life, erasing all black and white and leaving only vividness behind.

"I looked for you," he whispered.

"I know."

He smiled, drawing her hand so that it rested against his chest between them. "What I saw… You…"

"Shh…" She drew back, holding his gaze.

"But…"

Then she did what surely guaranteed his silence: she leaned in to press her lips delicately against his….

It was no more than a whisper, a light breeze blown over damp skin. But the impact was more powerful than the storm that had thrown his sailboat around like a toy and tossed him overboard. Pure need engulfed him as thoroughly as seawater, denying him breath and the ability to think beyond the desire to taste her again.

He flattened her hand against his chest then raised his fingers to her neck, lightly trailing the tips along the length, then back again as he leaned in for something a little more substantial.

Her eyes watched as he bent first one way, then the other, brushing his lips against hers before meeting them more fully.

She sighed, threading her arms under his and grasping his shoulders.

Whatever control he was hoping to wield fled with the last notes of the song on the wind and the feel of her body flush against his. He cupped the back of her neck and drew her closer still, drinking deeply of her damp mouth, unsure if it was her quickening of breath he heard or his own.

She was all sweet, hot woman to his hard, wanting man. In that moment, he knew she could ask anything of him, and he'd give it. It was a hell of a place for him to be, considering all he'd been through. But that's what made it all the more magical...

He slid his hands down to her hips, grasping them through the light fabric of her dress, feeling her shiver as he pressed his hardness against her softness. She gasped. He groaned and deepened their kiss.

Knowing she wanted him as bad as he wanted her was the most powerful aphrodisiac of all.

He drew his right hand along her bare shoulder, cupping her breast through her dress, finding the tip hard. He lightly pinched it, his mouth watering with the desire to kiss it. He reached behind her, found her zipper and then slowly tugged until the material of the front bowed outward. She caught it almost shyly, holding it against her.

So enchanting…

He took her hand in his and turned it over, pressing his lips to the middle of her palm, then moved it to her side, allowing him free access to the nipple even now pouting at him in the pale moonlight.

He'd seen her breasts the other morning, after the storm. He knew they were perfectly round, beautifully tipped. He hadn't dared try to touch them then. But now…

He rasped the pad of his thumb over the stiff flesh, then cupped her so he could lean down to run his tongue over the hard, puckered surface.

She moaned deep in her throat, leaning more heavily against him, her hands going to his shoulders as if afraid she might fall without him to steady her. He slid his other arm around her, as much to reassure her he wouldn't allow her to slip, as well as to keep her close.

He licked her leisurely, moving to her other breast before he pulled her nipple deep into his mouth, sucking hungrily.

She moved restlessly against him, her fingers entwining in his hair as if caught between wanting to pull him closer and push him away.

Holding her with his mouth, he moved his free hand down, finding the side slit in her dress and sliding his fingers inward toward the top of her inner thighs. The crotch of her panties was drenched with want.

He groaned. "Oh, God, you're so wet…."

She pulled his head up and kissed him deeply, thrusting her hips forward. It was an unspoken cry he was only too willing to answer.

He dipped his fingertip inside the edge of her panties, finding her perfectly bare and softer than anyone had a right to be. He worked his thumb inside the delicate fabric and then followed an invisible line down, delving the thick digit into her slick channel.

Her moan was anything but quiet as she collapsed against him, relying on him to hold her up. Her breathing came in quick, uncontrolled gasps as he rotated his thumb and thrust it deeply inside her, pressing on the back wall of her vagina. She bore down against him, pressing her clit against his wrist while he moved.

"Come for me, sweet Daphne," he whispered.

When she cried out a moment later, he knew she had....

DAPHNE HAD BEEN touched before, but never this powerfully....

She felt as substantial as the water she loved, flowing, rippling, completely at the mercy of currents beyond her control.

She rested her forehead against Kieran's shoulder, trying to catch her breath, attempting to process what had just happened, straining to hear the faint warning bell that sounded in the back of her mind....

She couldn't be sure what the bell heralded, but knew a pang of fear all the same.

"I want you…" Kieran whispered into her ear before sweeping her up into his arms.

She made a soft sound before cuddling closer to him.

She was barely aware of anything outside the feel of his arms around her as he took her inside the house. Within moments, they were in what she guessed was his bedroom, which faced the same balcony on which they'd been standing a short time before. Moonlight bathed the bed in a warm, yellow glow as he put her on her feet then kissed her deeply. She cradled his handsome face in her hands even as he freed her of her dress then worked to take off his tux.

Soon nothing separated them but air….

He groaned as he looked at her. "So, so beautiful."

He picked her up again to lay her on the bed, then stretched out beside her. She felt his hard length against her hip and instinctively reached out, encircling her fingers around him. So thick…so warm…

He kissed her deeply then stilled her hand with one of his own before working his knee between hers and then moving to lie on top of her, nudging her thighs farther apart.

He leaned back, gazing at her. She smiled softly and raised her head to kiss him again. Then she guided him to her, tilting her hips so that the tip of his erection pressed against her.

Calling on whatever self-control he still had, he took

a condom from the bedside drawer, sheathed himself, then slowly breached her entrance.

She barely heard his groan as she gasped, feeling as if she'd just gone up in flames....

5

Kieran held himself very still, afraid that if he moved, he'd spill his need into her before even fully entering.

The problem was, he couldn't control *her* movements. So when she slid up his length, his arms shook with the effort to ward off coming.

Sweet Lord, she felt so exquisitely good. He longed to please her in a way no one ever had, wanted this to last for as long as he could make it.

He slowly withdrew, to her soft objection, then surged into her to the hilt. Her back came up off the mattress, jutting her breasts forward. He stroked her again, then bent to take one of her nipples deep into his mouth. She moaned low in her throat, threaded her fingers through his hair, then pushed up until he sat back on his haunches and she straddled him, her ankles crossed behind him, her mouth fastening on to his, her arms around his neck. She rocked against him.

He grasped her hips, wanting to hold her still, yet mesmerized by her sensual movements.

Then he stopped fighting and went with the flow....

The moment he gave himself over to the connection with her, he transcended his concern of premature ejaculation and they moved as one, caressing, exploring, gasping, each moment better than the one before.

The pure, sweet, hot bond was beyond anything he could recall experiencing before. There was no awkwardness or fear or inhibition...merely a true sharing, enjoyment of each other and their bodies.

Her breathing quickened, her heightened state of awareness feeding his own. She leaned back on one arm, giving him free view of her luscious body. Her torso moved in a boneless, mesmerizing way that left him spellbound. She was part cowgirl, part exotic dancer, part something different, not of this world.

Something from the sea...a beautiful mermaid come to rob him of his soul.

She leaned in to cling to him, kissing him hungrily. He slid his fingers to her bottom, cupping her firmly, spreading her to deepen his strokes. She gasped, her mouth opening against his, her body stiffening except for the slick muscles surrounding him, which grasped him tightly as she climaxed.

As he helplessly followed, one word claimed every available space in his brain: *magic*.

A LOUD BANGING, a ringing and a voice broke Kieran's sleep...

He tried to wake from the dream, but yet wanted to stay right where he was. So nice, so sexy, so warm...

"Sir, you really need to get up now."

There was a nudge to the shoulder.

Kieran finally cracked open his eyelids to find the room flooded with sunlight. It took him a moment to realize that the dream hadn't been a dream at all, but reality.

He jackknifed to a sitting position, searching the bed next to him. She was gone.

"Sir?"

He blinked until Samuel, his house manager, came into view. "Where is she?"

"Sir?" Samuel said again. "I can't say as I know to whom you're referring. But your parents have arrived downstairs and are quite anxious to see you."

His parents…

His parents!

He sprang from the bed. Damn. He'd completely forgotten he was supposed to pick them up at the airport this morning. What time was it?

He began to put his tux pants back on, thought better of it, then grabbed a pair of jeans from a drawer instead. He moved to get a shirt from the closet only to bump into Sam who held one out.

"Thanks."

"Just part of the job."

Within thirty seconds he was down the stairs, an apology on his lips, to find his father bringing in luggage.

"Here, let me get that," he said.

"No, no, it's quite all right. As I told your houseman,

I find it therapeutic to move around a bit after being cooped up on a plane for so bloody long."

Kieran hugged his dad, who always appeared uncomfortable with such displays of affection but smiled nonetheless.

"And where's the missus. I assume that's why you slept in?" His dad's eyes sparkled. "The two of you have a good night."

Hell.

"Where's Mom?" Kieran asked, dodging the topic and going to look through the open door.

"She wandered off, in search of the loo..."

Kieran could only hope she didn't stumble across anything—or anyone—else...

DAPHNE COULDN'T HELP herself. When she'd awakened feeling such an all-encompassing sense of satisfaction, she'd decided a nice soak in a water-filled tub would be nice. Only, she hadn't dared do it in Kieran's master bath where he might come upon her. Instead, she'd chosen the ensuite in one of the nearby guest bedrooms that boasted a good-size Jacuzzi. She lay back, the nearby Bose radio tuned into a 50's satellite station, her fins hanging over the far side of the tub. It was almost instinctual. If she was in water, her fins followed.

Okay, she now understood why her mother might have chosen land over the sea. Last night...

Last night had been so...

She sighed and closed her eyes, leaving it there.

She knew soon she'd have to get out of this tub, call a taxi and head back home, but right now she was content to stay where she was, basking in all that was...

She smiled, realizing she was lazily drawing circles around her nipples.

Every part of her felt wondrously, gloriously alive. Even her scales now looked somehow more iridescent to her. She ran her hands down them, reveling in the texture, slowly flapping her fins.

The door opened....

At first Daphne was sure she was seeing things. Stuff like this didn't happen in real life.

She stared at the startled older woman with neat gray hair wearing a skirt suit, unsure what to say, unsure what to do.

The woman took the decision out of her hands. She screamed...

KIERAN AND HIS father heard the high-pitched shriek coming from upstairs.

"She probably spotted a spider," his father said in his usual droll tone.

Kieran had never heard a noise like that come from his mother, spider or no.

"I think we'd better—"

He didn't get a chance to finish as his mother came rushing down the stairs, looking awkward in her high heels as she took the steps.

"Careful!" he called, half afraid she'd fall.

She reached them, out of breath, pointing up the stairs. "There's a..."

"Is everything okay, madam?" Samuel asked as he came in from the kitchen.

"Of course, everything is not okay! There's a... There's a..."

Kieran nodded, gesturing for her to finish her sentence.

"Spider?" his dad offered.

"No!" She glared at him. "In the guest bathroom... In the tub..."

"A roach?"

Again his father was rewarded with one of his mother's icy stares.

Then it occurred to Kieran what could have possibly been in his tub.

As his parents argued back and forth, Kieran leaned closer to Sam. "Did you see a beautiful redhead leave this morning?"

"No, sir. I did not."

Oh, hell...

"Come on! If you don't believe me, come have a look for yourself!"

His mother began to lead the way back up the stairs.

His father sighed. "Do you have some newspaper or something we can roll up?"

"Right away, sir," Sam said.

Kieran dragged his feet as he followed his parents, his mind going over everything they might possibly see when they reached that bathroom door.

"It's a..." his mother continued, reaching the guest-bedroom door.

She grasped the knob of the bathroom door, squared her shoulders and thrust it open.

"Mermaid," she finally finished her sentence.

Kieran closed his eyes, half afraid to look.

"It's been confirmed. You are daft."

His father's comment encouraged him to open an eyelid. There was nothing in the room.

"But, I swear..."

His mother stepped inside the bathroom, then pointed to the tub that was nearly done draining of water.

"See! She was here!"

Sam came into the room with the rolled up paper his father had requested. He shared a look with Kieran.

"Ah, yes," he said. "You must be referring to Master Kieran's overnight guest...."

Everyone looked at him.

"Miss Moore," he said. "I'd almost forgotten."

"Overnight guest?" his mother asked. "You had a mermaid as an overnight guest?"

His father heaved a sigh. "Will you please stop this nonsense? There's no such thing as a mermaid."

Elizabeth ignored him and planted her hands on her hips. "Well, then, where is this guest now?"

"I daresay you've frightened her away," his father said. "If the spine scratching scream didn't do it, I'm sure the following witch hunt did."

"I believe Miss Moore has left the premises," Sam said.

Kieran wondered if that was true. Or was she hiding somewhere, waiting for them all to leave?

"Shall we retire to the front room?" Sam suggested. "You've just come from a long trip and I've prepared some refreshments."

Kieran made a mental note to give Sam a big bonus at month's end.

"That's it," his father said. "The trip must have made you daft."

"I'm not daft. I know what I saw."

"Well, then, maybe we should check one of the adjoining rooms. Perhaps we'll see Poseidon. Or Aphrodite. Or maybe the Loch Ness monster will make herself visible...."

Kieran watched them leave, his parents' fading bantering telling him when they'd reached the hall.

He turned back toward the empty tub. He leaned closer, spotting something shiny in the bottom. He fingered the object, then picked it up. It looked like a...

Scale.

He looked around, but there was no other sign of Daphne.

He slowly pocketed the scale, then followed on his parents' heels, reminding himself to have Sam give them another room...

6

OKAY, TWO UNIQUE experiences within a twelve-hour time span would be enough to throw anyone a little off kilter. At least, that's what Daphne told herself as the taxi dropped her off at her small house in Dolphin Way. The driver's openly curious look as she got out of the car in her evening gown, and holding her sandals, was nothing compared to what she'd been through, so she merely tipped him generously, smiled and closed the door.

She barely heard him drive away as she stood staring at the small, one-story bungalow that had been hers for the past eight years. Compared to the larger places on either side, it wasn't anything spectacular, but that had been fine with her. She hadn't needed anything big. She'd grown up in what she'd called The Hotel, finding little comfort in the cavernous areas and never-ending maze of rooms.

Funny that she should find the vast expanse of the sea far more welcoming.

She absently touched the For Sale sign bearing a Sold sticker on the front lawn and then walked to what was essentially the back door, since the front faced the beach and the Pacific. The title closing had taken place last week, and the new owners—a young couple with two kids—would be taking possession next week. Right after her rededication to the sea.

She let herself inside the house, put her human possessions down, slipped out of her dress and put on one of the many swimsuits all in the same color and style that she kept near the back door. Then moments later, she was walking into the Pacific, barely breaking her stride.

The instant she was immersed she dove deeper and kicked her legs together, more as one than two. By the third kick, scales fanned down from her waist, and by the fourth, fins gave her the speed she craved.

She wasn't sure how long she swam and was barely aware of where she was. All she knew was the desire for a change of scenery to allow her to process her emotions, put everything back into perspective.

Kieran.

Her scales instantly tingled and puffed out.

Wow…

The word caught and held in her mind. She could never have imagined feeling that…alive with anyone, much less a human.

Or perhaps his being human had nothing to do with it. Maybe he was her soul mate, as her mother occasionally called her father.

Speaking of parents, she winced as she remembered Kieran's mother's scream when she'd found her in the tub, indulging in a forbidden tail bath in a human household. She'd overheard his conversation with them in the foyer as she hurried down the back stairs, running into what she guessed was Kieran's house manager in the kitchen. They'd stared at each other and then he'd simply taken a look at her attire and said, "I'll have a taxi waiting for you around the east corner in five minutes. I'll make sure you're left alone back here until then."

She'd thanked him and then snuck from the house when she judged the time to be right.

She could only imagine what Kieran's mother thought of her. While his seeing her ranked as fantasy material, his mother was more inclined to think her part of a nightmare...

She knew a sinking sensation. If they were to meet in the real world, she was certain the woman would recognize her and there would be no smiles. To the contrary, she was relatively certain she'd earn another scream.

But Kieran...

She found herself smiling again and gave a watery sigh.

She slowed her speed, taking a look around. She wasn't far from the reef and the nearby caves of Nalisha where many of her kind lived a humanlike, underwater existence. She hadn't been consciously aware of her destination, but now that she was there...

The oldest of the school was Magda, one time known as Magdalena. Time had not been kind to the old mermaid; her scales were ragged, her body bloated, and the human part of her didn't look any better, so everyone called her Magda.

Still, she was long considered the elder and it was she who oversaw all ceremonies. She would be officiating Daphne's confirmation next week.

Daphne headed in the direction of her dwelling, unsurprised when Magda swam to the opening as if anticipating her visit.

"I've been expecting you."

"Oh?"

"I've been hearing rumors."

Daphne followed her inside when invited.

"Is it true you've become involved with a human?"

One of the many aspects of mermaid life that was very similar to human existence was the endless gossip. Until now, she'd managed to stay untangled in the sharp net. And while she could spend months trying to figure out who had seen her interaction with Kieran, what mattered in the end was someone had.

And he was the reason she'd sought out the elder's council.

"Yes. Yes, it is." She didn't feel the need to share the deep level of their interaction, but she suspected it was obvious. It was probably all over her like an oil slick.

She looked down at her gently waving fins. "I was hoping we might postpone my confirmation."

She hadn't been aware that's what she was going to request until she heard herself say the words.

Magda pretended interest in an electric eel that had just entered her cave.

Finally, she turned back toward Daphne, her gaze even. "No."

Daphne's stomach hurt. The thought that she might not see Kieran again after next week inspired a sadness deeper than any she'd felt before.

"Daphne, Fate's wheels have already begun turning. The ceremony is nothing more than a formality. Your responsibility to mermaidhood has already been established."

"I don't understand..."

"It's quite easy, actually. You made your decision at sixteen. And since then, you have spent more time in the sea than on land..."

She nodded solemnly.

"As a result, you probably found it more difficult and uncomfortable to achieve and maintain human form."

Yesterday, her transformation before going to her parents' had actually been painful. And she had recognized that changing had grown progressively harder over the past few months.

"Next week, you will lose your ability to transfigure altogether...."

Daphne had been aware of that. And only twelve short hours ago, she had eagerly looked forward to making the commitment.

Now, though...

Well, now she felt compelled to explore what was happening between her and Kieran.

And she couldn't do that in the short time they had together.

Nor could she do that as a mermaid.

"So you're saying that even if I chose not to go ahead with the ceremony, my fate is sealed."

"It's not a death sentence, Daphne. It's a privilege."

Why did she suddenly feel as if the former was closer to the truth?

"But there is one way."

Hope.

"You must marry this human before your confirmation."

She gasped. The mere prospect of wedding a man she had just met was more shocking than what she'd just learned about her fate. Mere hours ago, she'd been questioning what had been a steadfast, lifetime commitment. She couldn't possibly consider making a completely different one in the time she had left...

"I can't do that."

Was that a smug smile on the old mermaid's face?

It was gone before she could be sure.

"Then my suggestion would be for you stay away from this human," Magda said.

Daphne felt as if her heart had not merely cracked, but crumbled into dust. But that made no sense. She'd shared only one night with Kieran. Surely what she was feeling couldn't be true love. Not the kind her parents shared. Not the type that had compelled her mother to give up the sea for her father.

"Good luck," Magda said, effectively dismissing her.

"Thank you."

As she swam out of the dark cave, she couldn't help thinking she was going to need more than luck to see her through the hours and days ahead of her....

7

HIS PARENTS WERE NOT PLEASED.

That was the understatement of the century.

He could still hear his mother's gasp when he'd given her the news that not only wasn't Clarissa in the house, they were no longer married.

"What do you mean you're no longer married? You mean, you're…"

"What, Mother? Divorced?"

"Good God, boy, are you trying to send her into cardiac arrest?"

His father's rebuke had hit its intended target and he'd apologized.

Not that it helped anything. Elizabeth Morrison had taken the victim ball and run with it, making the next few hours a lesson in civility.

Finally, Samuel had rescued him by telling him he had an urgent call from the company.

He hadn't, of course. There had been nothing urgent in connection with the company in years.

But it had provided the excuse he needed to extricate himself from the insufferable situation and send his parents off on their own. Hopefully when he saw them later, his mother would have moved on to another topic…like how she always forgot how hot it was in Southern California and how could he stand it, anyway?

A short time later, he'd found himself standing outside the small house bearing a SOLD Realtor's sign. He'd had his attorney's office track Daphne down to this address, and he was hoping they'd have a chance to talk about what was going on between them.

Unfortunately, there had been no answer to his knocks. Not that he'd expected one. He understood last night had been a one-shot deal. For reasons he couldn't quite define, there was a certain…limited urgency to their relations. Once she was gone, he'd sensed he'd never see her again.

And seeing that Sold sign had merely driven that suspicion home.

Still, that didn't stop him from driving to the Newport Beach Marina, where he intended to take the schooner out and sail until he found her.

"Mr. Morrison?"

He was taking off his shoes and boarding the boat when he spotted the young, suited man advancing on him. "Yes?"

"This is for you."

The man held out a sealed envelope.

"Thank you…"

As the guy walked away, Kieran ran his hand through his hair and considered the object in his hands.

Items of this nature were never good.

He tore off the end of the envelope and shifted out the folded contents….

And felt like he'd just been sucker punched.

DAPHNE WAS AWARE of Kieran before she saw the hull of his sailboat slicing the sea's surface.

She stopped her manic, aimless swimming and stared up, watching as the boat slowed.

Was it possible he sensed her…?

She pushed upward, aiming for a spot some hundred feet away where she might get a glimpse of him, just a glimpse, without his seeing her. She didn't want to interact with him. She couldn't. But it wouldn't hurt to see him…

She slowly broke the surface, watching as the sailboat slowed to a dead stop in the water, the motors having propelled it rather than the sails. And there Kieran stood on the deck, shielding his eyes as he scanned the water.

Daphne ducked back beneath the waves, his instincts a little too uncanny for her liking.

Something broke the water. She looked to see that Kieran had dove in and was swimming in her direction.

She was shocked to the spot.

He reached her and motioned upward with his thumb.

She broke the surface with him.

"I knew it was you," he said. "I had to find you, had to see you...."

She was incapable of words. Incapable of movement. Incapable of doing anything but looking at his handsome face, the intensity of emotion in his expression.

He didn't even seem to care that while he labored to tread water, her tail allowed her to stay still with barely any action on her part.

He didn't seem to care she was a mermaid.

"What are you doing?" she whispered.

His grin warmed her more powerfully than the sun through clear waters.

"I had to see you."

All at once, Daphne was reminded of their all too brief time together, the memory of which she'd planned to wrap around her on cold nights. His kiss, his touch, his softly said words...

And now he was here, his mere presence promising that if she wanted more, it was there for the asking...

But she couldn't take it.

She began turning away.

"Please, don't go," he said, grasping her arm.

It would be as simple as sinking beneath the water's surface and swooshing her tail once to escape him forever. But in that one moment, she couldn't have moved if her life depended on it.

"I love you," he said.

KIERAN WOULDN'T HAVE believed the words had he not heard himself say them.

But once he had...

"I know it sounds silly," he said quickly. "I can't believe it's true myself."

The grin he felt split his face seemed to come from somewhere deep within.

"But it is."

She was no longer trying to move away from him. That was a good thing. Wasn't it?

"I feel stupid saying this," he said. "But from the first moment I spotted you... No, before then... It's like I *knew* you were there. That what I was looking for, seeking...it was out here somewhere. It was you."

He waited for skepticism to show on her face, but it didn't.

"You saw me, didn't you?" he asked, realization hitting him. "Before the night of that storm. You saw me."

She nodded almost imperceptibly.

"How long?"

She looked toward the boat, but didn't answer.

"How long?" he asked again, his fingers tightening slightly on the soft skin of her arm.

"The first day you came out."

His heart felt like it had doubled in size, which he knew was physically impossible.

Then again, so was the existence of mermaids.

"Please, Kieran," she said so softly it could have easily been mistaken for the wind. "Last night...was last night. You, me... We can't see each other again."

His grin faded.

"You have to promise me you won't come out here again, won't try to find me..."

What was she saying?

"I can't."

She grasped his forearms. "But you have to. Can't you see? We can't be together. This, whatever happened between us…happened. And it was wonderful. But it can't happen again. There's no future for us. No tomorrow. Nothing beyond last night."

"Why?"

Her expression was one of incredulity. She looked down at his legs, then her fins, then back up at him.

Kieran gazed deep into eyes that were the color of uncut emeralds, his need for her so consuming, he didn't care where they were or who might see them.

He grazed the back of his knuckles along her jaw, then curved his hand around her nape. Kissing her was one of the sweetest sensations he'd ever known. The thought that he'd never do it again…

He brushed his mouth lightly against hers, watching her expression go unchanged. Then he did it again, sampling the salt on her lips and dipping his tongue in for a more thorough taste.

Her eyes drifted closed, then opened again, a soft sigh bringing the tips of her breasts briefly against his chest. He deepened the kiss and drew her closer, aware she was solely responsible for keeping them afloat as his hands boldly explored her generous curves. She felt so good. He thought he could touch her for a million years and still want for more.

His fingers slid down her rib cage to her waist… reaching the point where skin turned to scale.

She caught her breath, her eyes watchful. He held her gaze as he skimmed his hands lower...

He wasn't sure what he'd expected. He was a lifelong fisherman and knew the texture of many different species of fish. But this, her...

So silky...

So smooth...

So inviting...

He grasped her hips, marveling at the toned muscle, the fanning of her scales, even as she moved to keep their heads above water.

Then his touch grew bolder still....

DAPHNE GASPED, GOING still as Kieran probed areas she'd never dreamed he'd dare....

They both dipped under the waves before she caught herself and brought them both back above the water. She expected to see panic on his handsome face at going under. Instead, he gazed at her with the same warm, sexy intensity, completely trusting her as he kissed her again.

She moaned deep in her throat, threading her fingers through his wet hair and launching a hungry assault on his mouth. His hands explored and stroked areas of her that weren't human, igniting sensations that were so entirely new to her, she was forced outside her normal boundaries of control.

He wasn't...

There wasn't a chance...

No way was he...

His fingers stroked her most delicate parts and she went completely boneless against him, somehow managing to keep them afloat but having no idea how since she completely surrendered to his intimate touch.

That he would want to feel her like this touched her in ways that transcended the sexual and demonstrated the velocity of the sentiment he'd declared.

Then he was entering her…

She was incapable of movement, marveling at the way he filled her in her current form. If last night had been beyond phenomenal, this…

This…

He moved his hips, stroking her.

"So beautiful," he whispered into her ear.

Everything Daphne had ever believed suddenly went up in smoke. Her internal muscles clutched him, her external body trembled and shook…

The low, animalistic sound that erupted from his throat communicated his own climatic state.

She held him tightly, her body going rigid.

They slid beneath the waves, a single entity rather than two, completely joined, together.

And she knew she was now bound to this man in a way that had nothing to do with physical ropes, but with all-encompassing love….

"I'm willing to do whatever it takes to make this work…"

Kieran's words were barely audible to himself over

the sound of the waves gently lapping against their spent bodies.

He hadn't known a moment of fear as they sank into the water, joined in a way he suspected not many would ever achieve, the sea around them throbbing with life.

Then she'd brought them to the surface again and they held each other tightly.

"I can't imagine never touching you again," he said. "Kissing you…"

He pressed his mouth against hers.

"Making love to you…"

She made soft sounds as they kissed.

He reluctantly drew back, holding her gaze.

"Please tell me there's a chance. I would do anything…"

She didn't say a word for a long moment. And he found a glimmer of hope there.

"Anything…"

I WOULD DO anything for love, but I can't do that.

Hours later, Kieran stood on the deck of his gently swaying sailboat staring off into the sunset, for the first time not staring at the water, or the horizon. Not seeing much of anything at all, really.

Marriage…

He tried to make sense of his conversation with Daphne. The one they'd shared just a short while ago right where he was standing. Where she had agreed to join him when he could no longer tread water. She'd remained in her natural form, her breasts covered by her burning red hair, her tail shimmering in the golden light.

She'd said something about confirming her commitment to the sea…and the only way out of it was to marry before next week.

It would have been easier if she'd told him the moon was about to sink into the Pacific right where his boat was.

Marriage…

So much for being willing to do whatever it took.

The corner of the envelope he'd been handed earlier flapped in the light evening breeze. He edged it out from the brass paperweight holding it under the steering wheel and took out the papers again.

At first, he'd believed it was his final divorce decree, come a few days early.

Instead the documents informed him that his partner was suing for control of the company, on the grounds of Kieran's mental incompetence.

That made twice in six months that two of the people closest to him had betrayed him. He couldn't trust anyone.

So how could he possibly marry Daphne?

He wasn't sure how long he stood there, contemplating everything that had transpired in the past twenty-four hours, questioning his sanity as surely as Mike had, contemplating his life up until this point.

It was dark and the moon was high in the sky by the time he finally turned to head back into port. He was no closer to making sense of things than he had been three hours earlier. And he harbored the deep sensation that he wouldn't understand much anytime soon.

8

"WHAT DO YOU MEAN BY THIS?" Kieran slapped the tattered legal documents on his partner's desk at Morrison and Dunlop five days later.

Mike sat back in his chair. "Finally, a reaction."

"Piss off." Keiran paced across the well-appointed office in San Clemente with the view of the Pacific but too far away to smell it.

The ultimate in ironies.

He'd barely slept, barely eaten, and had all but pushed his parents aside, leaving them to entertain themselves for the most part, incapable of more than coffee with them in the mornings and after dinner. And even then, he'd been so zoned out that even his mother had taken a break from her usual obsessing to obsess over him.

He was a mess. He shouldn't even be here. He'd told himself he wouldn't confront Mike until he'd reestablished his equilibrium. Got some sleep. Put himself back to rights.

The problem was, he was starting to believe he was never going to achieve that.

He faced his onetime friend. "Explain."

Mike grinned. "Are you going to sign off on those papers?"

"Are you out of your damned mind?"

Mike got up and rounded the table, extended his hand. "Hello, Kieran. Good to see you again."

He took the hand but squeezed it to the point of pain. "I'm about two breaths away from laying you flat."

"Good."

He released Mike's hand. "Stop with the riddles and tell me what's going on."

Mike slapped him on the back and led him toward the small conference table in the corner with a killer view. "What's going on is that I've been waiting for you to snap out of this miserable state you've been in for the past six months."

"This has nothing to do with my divorce."

Mike offered him coffee but he refused. His friend poured them both a cup anyway, handing Kieran one as he sat down at the table. "It has everything to do with your divorce."

Kieran rubbed his forehead absently. Nothing made sense. It didn't help that his friend was being as clear as the coffee in his hand.

"She's not worth it."

Kieran squinted.

"But this really isn't about her, is it? This is about what she did."

"And what you did."

"What did I do?"

"You betrayed me. Just as surely as she did."

"No, buddy. I didn't betray you. I did what I had to do to bring you back from the brink of whatever you were ass-deep in the middle of."

Kieran thought back to the time when Clarissa had first left him. When he'd made radical changes in his life.

Had he been depressed?

Despondent?

"You didn't even offer up a token fight," Mike said, leaning back and crossing his ankle over his knee. "That's not the Kieran I know."

He grimaced and took a sip from his mug, although he remained standing.

"The guy I know would have raked her ass over the coals but good."

He considered him for a long moment. "And that's what you want me to do with you? Fight you?" He nodded toward the papers sitting in the middle of the desk.

"In a word—yes."

It made a backward kind of sense. Present him with a challenge, a violation of trust, in essence bait him into a fight.

"And if I hadn't fought?"

The smile disappeared from Mike's face. "Then we would have had a problem...."

"You would have gone forward with the action?"

His friend fell silent for long moments, pondering the question. "I don't know. I really hadn't thought that far ahead." He met his gaze. "All I knew was I had to do something."

Neither of them said anything, merely stared at each other.

"I felt like I was losing you, brother."

Mike's quietly said words hit him more profoundly than any physical punch.

Kieran felt himself smiling. "So, I guess I should be thanking you for serving me court papers, then?"

His friend threw back his head and laughed. "Yeah. I guess you should." He stretched out a leg and pushed out the chair in front of him. "Now, sit down and tell me if you've seen this mermaid of yours again…"

DAPHNE WAS MERE hours away from confirmation and was overcome with anxiety.

She swam aimlessly and then traded her fins for legs, visiting her old house on the shore one last time.

At least, that's what she told herself. Her motivations went much deeper.

Kieran hadn't been back…

Pain so acute it was nearly impossible to breathe shredded her insides as she recalled her last conversation with him on his schooner.

"I can't…"

Those two words echoed through her mind again and again until she was sure she would go insane.

She had never intended to share Magda's words.

Share her own misgivings about her confirmation decision. But he had been so earnest when he'd jumped into the sea after her. When he'd held her as if afraid if he let her go, he might never see her again.

When he'd told her that he loved her...

Her heart beat an ache so consuming it robbed her of thought.

A car horn sounded.

She looked up, hope swelling, from where she fingered the scalloped lace edge of the living-room curtains. She'd found them at an antiques shop, and had fallen in love with them on sight. But she intended to leave them with the house. After all, what would she do with them in the sea?

But it wasn't Kieran: it was her mother.

She'd known Cecelia was coming, of course. In fact, she herself had arranged for what amounted to her final celebratory brunch.

Still, she couldn't help wishing it were Kieran...

"You look pretty," her mom said, taking in her simple linen skirt and jacket.

"Thanks," she answered absently as she climbed into the car and closed the door.

"I was thinking we'd hit that place a little ways up the coast. The one that specializes in crepes?"

Daphne nodded.

She stared through the window at the rolling waves, the never-ending sea of blue, feeling detached somehow...not a part of it...

Not a part of anything.

"Your dad will be meeting us there."

"Huh? Oh. Good." She tried for a smile.

She knew what she was looking for. And as they neared the Newport Beach Marina where she knew *Come Sail Away* was docked, she couldn't help seeking out signs of Kieran. She saw none.

"So today's the big day, huh?"

She looked at her mother. There seemed to be a delay between whatever she said and Daphne's ability to process it.

"Yes," she said finally.

She looked away from Cecelia's probing gaze.

"I wish your father and I could attend."

"Me, too."

She didn't realize her mother had stopped the car until the engine was completely off.

Cecelia had pulled off onto an overlook, as traffic continued to flow on the highway behind them.

"Okay, what's wrong?"

"What? Nothing. Everything's fine." She tried for a smile again and failed miserably. "This is the day I've been looking forward to all my life."

"Yes…"

"The sea is all I've ever wanted. To confirm my love for it today is nothing short of amazing."

"Uh-huh."

"If I'm feeling a little emotional about it all, that's only natural, right?"

"Yes."

She bit hard on her bottom lip, feeling ridiculously near tears. And joy had nothing to do with them.

"Now that you've told me what you're trying to convince yourself of, I think it's time you shared the truth."

The truth...

What was that?

She wasn't even sure.

"What if I wanted to become a mer...person? A merman?" Kieran's words burned her ear.

They'd been sitting on the deck of the schooner, the sun bright, the breeze warm, his declaration of love filling her inside and out.

Had that really only been last week? It seemed years ago. Yet just like yesterday.

In response to his question, she'd merely smiled.

One wasn't made a mermaid...she was born one. So Kieran's becoming a merman wasn't an option.

"And even if you could, would you want to?" she'd asked.

Not many would. Most born with the option chose not to follow the sea path. And while she'd never had the conversation with a human, she imagined that most would find the idea ludicrous.

But the expression on Kieran's face had been so earnest, so enchanting, she'd fallen a little deeper in love with him.

"Yes," he'd answered unequivocally.

She'd believed him.

His openness had allowed her to also believe that

perhaps she should consider the option Magda had offered.

So she had.

And he'd snapped shut on her tighter than a clam on feeding day.

"I can't..."

There they were again. Those two words. The ones that had haunted her ever since.

She'd experienced such an overwhelming sense of embarrassment, of shame, she'd just wanted to slink back into the water and drown.

Of course he couldn't marry her; he didn't even know her.

And she didn't know him.

It had been ridiculous to even, for the briefest of moments, entertain thoughts otherwise.

But he'd said he loved her.

"Daphne?"

Her mother's voice slowly drew her back to the here and now.

"The truth," she reminded her.

And, with a cloud of emotion choking her, Daphne shared it.

9

IT MADE NO SENSE. Then again, little about his life seemed to make sense right now.

Kieran sat with his parents on the patio back at his house, thinking of his conversation with Mike. His partner wanted Kieran to return to work at least part time. Oh, the company was doing fine, but it would do infinitely better if he returned to a more hands-on position, Mike argued, seeing as he had always been the eyes and ears, watching for opportunities and picking up on trends and information others missed.

Kieran hadn't promised anything, but his friend's offer and the way he'd gone about making it did capture his attention.

But perhaps not solely in the way Mike likely intended.

Then again, he was going to need something to occupy his time. After last week, well, he didn't expect to be spending much time on his boat. Even if he did, he knew he'd forever be looking for Daphne. And he'd forever be left trying to fill the gaping hole in his chest that salt water would only exacerbate.

He knew he'd never find her again. Not after what he'd said. What he'd done. In the moment, he'd been so fixated on his knee-jerk reaction to her proposal, he hadn't really noticed her response. Now, well, now thorns pierced his stomach, remembering the pain on her beautiful face.

Her expression had gone from one of pure bliss to heartbreak within a span of a few minutes.

The truth was, while he hadn't planned on falling in love with anyone, he had.

So why had he shut her down when she'd made her proposal?

All he could remember thinking, on the heels of receiving those legal documents from Mike, was how could he possibly trust anyone? He'd already been betrayed by the two closest people in his life.

That thought had springboarded into doubt about himself. If he couldn't trust his wife or best friend, how could he possibly trust himself? Trust that what he was feeling was real?

Trust that *she* was real?

He absently rubbed the pearl in his pocket, thinking of the papers he received yesterday making his divorce final.

"So I do hope you're planning to spend some time with us today, seeing as our flight leaves later this evening," he heard his mother say.

She'd actually been saying a lot, but he had his antenna tuned in on only those parts of her monologue that concerned him. Oh, he heard her opinions about the gaudiness of Hollywood, the place they'd gone yesterday and how everything translated so much better on film than in real life.

But it was her take on smells that had nearly pulled him into a conversation he wasn't really interested in having.

"Urine. It's everywhere. I don't know how you stand it," she'd insisted. It had been one of her more interesting comments.

Now, he rubbed his forehead and answered her.

"What's on the agenda?" he asked, glancing around once again.

He couldn't see the sea from here on the patio. Instead, lush greenery surrounded them, providing a natural wall between them and the world.

Trouble was he didn't want to be separated from it.

"Your father and I are planning to do some shopping at that new mall…"

He grimaced. *Shopping* was one of the trigger words that made him zone out.

Yes, he understood he saw his parents only a few times a year.

Yes, he understood they'd come all this way to see him and they wanted to spend time with him.

Yes, he understood he was being a real heel for avoiding their company.

But all he could think about was the fact that today was the day Daphne would rededicate herself to the sea.

When she'd choose to become a mermaid forever.

"Kieran, are you even listening to me?"

He heard his father sigh. "Leave the boy be, Elizabeth. Can't you see he's got something on his mind?"

"Yes, well, if he shared it, maybe it wouldn't be such a burden."

"Well, I suppose if he'd wanted to, he would have already."

While his parents' conversation played out around him, it was Mike's words that trailed through his mind.

"So, you love her."

It was a statement rather than a question.

And it was truer than any statement he'd ever uttered.

"I know...after what Clarissa did, I swore I'd never let another woman in. Never fall in love again."

Until he met Daphne...

It should have struck him as odd that he was discussing his life with a mermaid with his best friend, but it didn't. He and Mike went back to the tooth fairy and Santa Claus days. And they'd certainly shared more than their share of bizarre stories over the years.

Granted, none had been as unique as this one...

Hell, he wouldn't have blamed Mike if he'd gotten him certified and taken over control of the company.

"So what's the problem, then?" he'd asked. "Beyond the obvious? You know, like how exactly you go about having sex with a woman who is half fish..."

What was the problem, indeed...

Silence.

In that one moment, no one spoke—not even his mother—and no other sounds could be heard.

Only the question resonated in his mind.

Yeah, what *was* the problem?

DAPHNE AND HER MOM sat in silence. At some point, they'd left the car and moved to a bench overlooking the sea that had played such a significant role in both of their lives.

"So," her mother said softly.

Daphne looked down at her legs left bare by the short skirt she'd chosen. She'd never really appreciated them. They'd always just been there when she was in human form. But when Kieran had touched her, run his fingers over her calves, then upward toward her inner thighs...

She shivered in remembrance. When he'd touched her, she hadn't felt like a mermaid or human, she'd merely...felt.

Felt beautiful...

Felt wanted...

Felt loved...

"The man we're talking about. Is he the one from the party? Kieran Morrison?" her mother asked.

Daphne nodded without hesitation. The time for secrets had long since come and gone.

"Do you love him?"

Daphne looked at her.

What could she say? They'd known each other one night.

Still, she knew with her every molecule that she did.

She nodded again, the light wind adding to the tears in her eyes.

"He's all I think about, all I want…"

"Over and above the sea?"

Daphne looked out at the rolling waves, watching gulls dive and dolphins arc.

She nodded again. "Over and above everything."

They drifted back into silence again as Daphne tried to consider the life that was stretched out before her. But she was incapable of looking beyond the painful beating of her heart.

She glanced at her mother to find her watching her… and smiling.

"What?"

Cecelia shook her head and reached out to tuck a strand of blowing hair behind her ear. "Nothing. Seeing you like this, it reminds me of when I fell in love with your father."

"Yes, but Dad loved you back."

She expected to see pity on her mother's face. Rather, her smile never wavered. "When's the last time you saw him?"

The question surprised her. "Right after he said he couldn't marry me."

"Couldn't. Not wouldn't."

Daphne raised a hand. "What does it matter?"

"Oh, darling girl, it matters more than anything…"

"WHERE ARE YOU going now?" Kieran's mother asked.

"To correct the biggest mistake of my life."

Kieran didn't wait to hear her response. Not that it mattered. He was through the house and into his car before he even finished the sentence.

What had he been thinking?

Why had he pushed away the only thing that had made sense in his life in a long, long time?

Denied the best thing that had ever happened to him?

He had to force himself not to drive too recklessly as he headed the three miles to the marina and the schooner. He didn't how he was going to find her, only knew that he had to. Any way he could.

He didn't care what he had to do. Or how long it took.

He only hoped it wasn't too late…

What time was it? Had she said what time her confirmation was?

Where would it be?

He double-parked the car in the marina lot. Let them tow him, he didn't care. Then he rushed up the docks, climbed onto the *Come Sail Away* without removing his shoes and immediately began freeing her from her moorings.

Daphne…

Her name was like a song in his ears. So sweet… So irresitible…

If he couldn't have her, couldn't see her again, he didn't know what he'd do…

Within minutes, he was steering his way through the no wake zone, then fired up the engines the instant he hit open water. His destination was the place he'd seen her that first time.

He hoped it wasn't too late....

10

As HER MOTHER pulled up into the marina parking lot, Daphne spotted the schooner, sailing off.

"Kieran!" she called, only half out of the car.

She hadn't planned to do it. Hadn't even been sold on her mother's idea to look him up, learn the nature of his true emotions.

She was forced to admit there was no way for him to contact her, even if he wanted to, outside of taking *Come Sail Away* out to sea.

Which is exactly what he was doing now....

She ran past where his double-parked car was being considered by marina employees and off onto the dock. Only, he hadn't heard her and she watched as he switched into high gear, the engines churning out sea water behind it.

"Is that him?" her mother asked, catching up with her.

"Yes..."

"Do you think he's going after you?"

Daphne looked at her. She knew he was.

She spotted a small skiff nearby that someone had just pulled into a slip.

Daphne didn't think twice. She made a beeline for the boat, untying it and starting the motor before the older, slower moving owner could do much more than shout after her as she made her apologies.

She waved at her mother who stood looking after her in concern.

As soon as she was out of the no-wake zone, she hit the engine, going in the same direction Kieran had. But rather than continuing the boat chase, she killed the motor and jumped overboard, knowing she could beat any engine.

Fully immersed, she dove and began kicking her legs....

Only, there was no change.

She kicked harder.

Still, nothing.

She came to a dead stop under water, staring at where her legs were still legs.

How was that possible?

She concentrated, and experienced the pain of transformation she'd been feeling more and more lately...

She looked down. Still, nothing.

Not only that, but her lungs were protesting the lack of air.

A pang of panic shot through her.

She kicked up toward the surface, breaking it and gasping for air.

What was happening? Why hadn't she changed? Magda had told her she was essentially a mermaid for life, with or without the confirmation ceremony, unless she married.

So why was she still human?

She glanced in the direction Kieran's boat had gone. How could she go after him now?

She glanced at where the skiff rolled on the waves a short distance away and made her way toward it. The exercise was harder than she would have anticipated and it took her a good five minutes before she was safely in the boat.

Finally, she was once again speeding in the direction Kieran had gone.

There!

She shouldn't have been surprised to find him in the same spot he'd first seen her. The schooner was at a standstill and he was on the deck, his back to her.

She knew a moment of panic.

"No!" she called out.

Like her shout at the marina, this one went unheard. She didn't stand a chance against the boat motor and distance.

Twenty yards... Eighteen... Fifteen...

She watched in horror as he leaped off the deck of the boat, disappearing into the waves on the other side.

Her heart felt as if it were trapped inside the skiff's propellers.

Now what did she do?

KIERAN SANK LOWER and lower, avidly searching the depths of the sea around him for signs of Daphne. He didn't know how, but he sensed she knew of his presence.

Lower and lower...

The water began getting darker and his clothes no longer felt light but heavy against his skin.

No Daphne.

He'd been a competitive swimmer in school and knew how to conserve his energy and his breath. But it had been a long time since he'd swum in any capacity, much less competitively.

He looked up at the water's surface. It seemed suddenly so far away.

Another glance around, nothing. Daphne was nowhere to be found.

He began kicking toward the surface, reminding himself panic was his worst enemy right now. Setting a nice, even pace would win the day.

The only problem was, he hadn't thought this all the way through.

His clothes clung to him like heavy chains, his shoes leaden weights.

He knew it was too late to try to take off anything. He needed to keep making for the surface.

He stretched up his arms, reaching...

Too far...

Too deep...

He wasn't going to make it...

A sound filled his ears. He looked to see someone

else had jumped into the water near him, some twenty feet up and sinking fast.

Daphne.

He smiled and swam faster, taking in the long line of her legs, the cloud of her long hair.

Long legs…

He tried to make sense out of the words.

Where were her fins?

She reached him and they clutched each other, him pulling her close. Love filled him inside and out.

She pulled away and nodded toward the surface.

He shook his head. He wasn't going to make it.

Still, he couldn't help the feeling of calm that had taken hold of him. It might be his end, but it didn't have to be hers.

He motioned for her to go.

She wildly shook her head.

Together.

He made out the word she mouthed easily enough.

But he knew that only one of them was going to get out of this alive. And he'd prefer that it be her.

Go.

He mouthed his own word.

She shook her head again and grasped his arms, kicking strongly. But she couldn't be that close and be effective.

He shoved her away.

Go!

She held on to him tighter.

Their gazes locked.

He knew, in that one moment, that if he didn't try, she would drown right there with him.

They both began swimming toward the surface.

Only, it was truly too late.

Blackness flickered across the screen of his mind, before going completely blank....

No!

Fear struck Daphne to the core as Kieran's eyes drifted closed and he went limp, sinking deeper.

She pulled on him and kicked, but it was no use. They were too far from the surface for her to pull him.

If at any time she wished she could change into a mermaid, it was now. Only, she couldn't.

Still, she wasn't ready to give up...

She frantically looked around, trying to summon help. Surely not all of her mermaid abilities had disappeared. A friendly dolphin would be perfect right about now. Or even a fellow mermaid.

Nothing.

It was getting darker.

She kicked harder, but her lungs were beginning to burn.

When had she become completely human? And why?

Had simply longing to trade her fins for legs in order to be with the man she loved, been enough for her to lose her privileges? If so, why hadn't she been told?

Her heart grew heavy in her chest. Not at the prospect of physical death. But of the death of what had just begun to grow between them.

Such love…

Such passion…

Such promise…

She held Kieran close and closed her eyes.

The jerk on her arm was so insistent and unexpected she opened her mouth and took in water.

She stared at the person doing the grabbing.

Mom?

Cecelia clutched Daphne's jacket in one hand, Kieran's shirt in her other, and pushed upward, her long, strong tail giving her the power she needed to propel them both to the ocean's surface.

Daphne sputtered and coughed, staring at her mother in shock even as she struggled to keep Kieran afloat. With Cecelia's help, they got him back to the schooner where Daphne performed CPR on him.

"Please," she whispered between aspirations, afraid it was too late.

"He'll come back," her mother said.

Daphne met her gaze, hoping she was right.

Finally, Kieran coughed up the water he'd taken in and blinked his eyes open.

Daphne held him so tightly she couldn't breathe.

And was suddenly afraid he couldn't, either.

"Sorry," she said softly, releasing her hold. "Are you going to be okay?"

He nodded, continuing to cough as he lifted himself to his elbows and leaned to the side.

As much as she hated to, she moved slightly away from him to look to where her mother had gone back into the water.

"You. Me. We need to have a talk," she said.

Her mother merely smiled. "I look forward to it."

Then she sank beneath the surface and swam away.

"Gardenias…"

She looked back at Kieran, who she decided must be hallucinating. "What?"

He smiled at her. "You saved my life. Again."

She held him close, held him tight, knowing that whatever she might have done for him, he'd done ten times over for her.

And she looked forward to making him understand that in every way possible….

Epilogue

A month later...

"I STILL CAN'T BELIEVE you kept it from me all these years," Daphne said as she and her mother skimmed through the sweet blue waters of the Pacific under the hull of the schooner. "The fact that you could still transform."

"I still can't believe you bought Magda's tale. She's been trying to sell that story forever."

Daphne couldn't believe it, either.

"And I won't even mention what you did to yourself that day."

Daphne couldn't think about that awful, humbling stretch in the water, when she'd nearly lost Kieran, without feeling that blinding fear all over again.

Had she really been so overwhelmed she'd allowed herself to believe she'd lost her power?

Yes, she had.

She was happy to say she'd quickly overcome that, however.

"Why didn't you tell me?" she asked her mother.

She hadn't had an opportunity to really talk to her mother, since that day. She'd been preoccupied with trying to absorb all that had happened and adjusting to her new life—not only accepting Kieran's proposal of marriage, but getting married a week ago at a small ceremony at her parents' home, attended by only a handful of family and friends.

And, of course, there'd been the weeklong honeymoon on the schooner where they had to remind themselves to take breaks from lovemaking to eat.

"About Magda?" her mother asked.

"No. I mean, yes, that, too, but mostly about your remaining a mermaid."

Cecelia didn't speak for a long time and their pace slowed.

"Your father and I talked long and hard about this when you were born. Of course, he knew what I was, what I am." She smiled. "But it was important to us both that you be allowed to make your own decisions."

"But how could I make an informed one if I was lacking important key information?"

"But you had all the information you needed."

"Did I? Because I'm thinking I didn't. Had I known I could remain a mermaid…"

"A swim every now and again does not a mermaid make."

"Yes, but you're not completely human, either."

Had she known the decision she'd made when she was sixteen and the confirmation ceremony were mere traditions and not true mandates, well, things would have unfolded much differently.

Of course, considering what had transpired in the time since, perhaps it wasn't a good idea to contemplate changing a single thing.

"Maybe…" her mother admitted.

They shared a smile and then whipped around a bit, chasing each other then circling back to *Come Sail Away,* where both of their husbands waited.

Daphne went first, transforming and grabbing a waiting towel before climbing up the ladder. Her mother followed a moment later.

On deck, she slipped into a swimsuit under the towel. Kieran came up behind her and kissed her neck.

"Nice swim?"

"Very." She smiled and held his head against her before turning and kissing him.

She shivered in instant need.

"Not in front of the parents, please," she heard her father say from the bow where they would be having breakfast.

Daphne kissed Kieran again in a way that was borderline parent proper.

"Payback for all the times I had to watch you and Mom growing up," she told her dad.

She gave her husband a nice butt grab for good measure, earning her a laugh from her mother and a groan from her father.

She took the juice and coffee carafes from Kieran and put them on the table. "What's for breakfast?"

"So long as it's not fish, I'm in," her mother said.

They all laughed.

"I'm about to make the eggs now. Want to give me a hand?" Kieran asked.

"Love to."

They began moving toward the hatch.

"We'd like to eat sometime this morning," her father called out.

Kieran chuckled and the moment they were below deck, grabbed Daphne and kissed her senseless.

She leaned against him, gasping for air, wondering if there would ever come a time when he wouldn't affect her so powerfully. When one of his kisses wouldn't be enough to make her forget who she was and what she was doing.

She wanted nothing more than to edge him back toward the main cabin, push him to the bed that bore the pearl, her pearl, in the middle of the custom-made headboard, straddle him until her thighs ached and she was incapable of doing anything but lying across the bed whispering incoherently.

He slowly ended the kiss and pressed his nose against hers. "Eggs."

"Mmm…yeah. Eggs."

He groaned and kissed her again. "Remember the other day…? I want to try it again…"

She smiled at him suggestively. "Later."

She knew exactly what he was talking about. They'd

made love while she'd been a mermaid and it had been...

Mmm...

She lost herself in his kiss, looking eagerly forward to not just tonight, but tomorrow, and the years after that....

Happily ever after.

Now *that* was her idea of a fairy tale....

* * * * *

KATE HOFFMANN

Off the Beaten Path

1

GRETA ADLER QUICKLY flipped through the slides for the client presentation, saying a silent prayer that everything was in order. Sunrise Airlines would be a perfect client for the agency—and she'd be the perfect senior art director for the account…once they got the account.

Her stomach fluttered nervously. She'd been aiming for the promotion for months now, but it never seemed to be the right time. This presentation was her chance to show Rich Johnson, Bob Jacobs and the rest of the management team at Johnson-Jacobs Advertising that she was ready for more responsibility.

Rubbing her eyes, she fought a wave of exhaustion. She and Alex Hansen, the account manager, had fine-tuned the details of the multimedia show until the wee hours the previous night and she'd only managed an hour or two of sleep before she jumped out of bed and headed for the office.

"Just don't screw up," she whispered to her laptop,

"or I will throw you into rush-hour traffic in downtown Denver and you'll be nothing more than scrap metal."

"That's the way to keep your electronics in line. I put my iPod in the freezer when it acts up."

Greta turned to see Alex enter the conference room. She ignored the tiny thrill that raced through her at the sight of him, writing it off to nervousness. As always, he was dressed beautifully, in an expensive suit and silk tie. Greta thought Alex Hansen was by far the sexiest man on staff at Johnson-Jacobs Advertising, and every other woman on the twenty-seventh floor was in complete agreement.

Alex placed his hand on her back and rubbed gently. "Don't worry," he said softly. "We're ready."

Greta drew a ragged breath. His touch sent a rush of warmth through her body. This was crazy! Where was this sudden attraction coming from? They'd been friends for seven years—well, seven years minus one night of drunken passion. And until recently, she'd never felt anything more than warm affection for him.

"I'm—I'm just tired," she said. That was it. Exhaustion was scrambling her emotions. "Maybe we should transfer the file over to your laptop. Mine is so temperamental."

"Don't worry," Alex repeated with a grin. He stood beside her and counted through the presentation folders. "Everything will be fine. We're ready. We've covered all our bases and they'd be crazy not to go with us."

Greta nodded. She could always depend on him to calm her nerves, no matter what the situation. In truth, maybe she'd come to depend on him a bit too much. After watching her parents' marriage dissolve in front of her, she'd been reluctant to put complete trust in any man. But with Alex she had a loyal friend and a dependable man. He'd been with her through unwelcome rodents, plumbing disasters, weeklong bouts of influenza and a variety of breakups.

They'd started at the agency together seven years ago—she right out of art school and he out of an MBA program at Colorado State. A casual acquaintance at work had grown into a playful camaraderie, which had blossomed into a mostly platonic relationship that their friends still questioned.

It was all very simple. She just wasn't his type and he wasn't hers. Alex liked tall, leggy blondes and she was small and brunette. And Greta still searched for that one perfect man who was looking for a real relationship, not just a few weeks of great sex followed by a quick breakup.

Two single people of the opposite sex could be best friends if there was no reason to become lovers. It had worked until one drunken night four years ago. But that slip had been an aberration, a mistake they both regretted and quickly put behind them.

Even though that night was just a hazy memory, Greta had found herself trying to recall it again and again lately. Over the past year, something had changed. With every woman that waltzed into Alex's life, she felt increasing pangs of jealousy. And she didn't think it was entirely one-sided. Alex had turned a little bit more possessive lately, too. There had been moments when Greta had questioned whether they were slowly growing apart as friends or whether something fundamental had shifted between them.

Maybe she was finally ready to admit the reality of their situation. Sooner or later, Alex would meet the woman of his dreams and she'd be left out in the cold. She couldn't imagine any new bride appreciating her husband having a female best friend.

"Aren't you nervous?" she said.

Alex leaned close, playfully bumping her shoulder. "You've done a really good job, Adler. You deserve a lot of credit. And I think you're going to get exactly what you want."

"A rich boyfriend with a private jet and a vacation home in Belize?" she asked.

"That's what you want?" Alex asked.

"Every girl wants that," she murmured. "That and zero-calorie ice cream, designer shoes that don't pinch and hair that fixes itself in the morning."

"I was talking professionally. I think they're going to promote you to senior art director."

"Really," Greta said, grabbing his arm. "And you know this how?"

"Because Bob Jacobs called me into his office an hour ago and asked if I thought you deserved it. I said yes. I told him you've been ready since you handled the Besconi Pasta presentation."

"Thank you," Greta cried. She threw her arms around his neck and gave him a fierce hug. He was such a good friend and she'd be a fool to change that now. But as she drew back, her cheek brushed against his. They froze, their lips just a few inches apart.

Greta's heart slammed in her chest and she felt her knees wobble. It wouldn't take much to kiss him, she mused. All she'd have to do was just...

"No problem," Alex murmured. He gently stepped back, his hands smoothing along her upper arms.

Blood rushed to Greta's cheeks and she laughed. "You wanted to kiss me, didn't you?" Okay, so maybe that was wishful thinking.

Alex gasped. "What?"

"Don't try to deny it. For a second there, you forgot who I was and you were ready to dive right in for a little action." She sent him a playful look and tried to calm her racing heart. This was the way they communicated, teasing and taunting each other. Never really saying how they felt about each other.

"Well, aren't you full of yourself. You're on the verge of a promotion and all of a sudden you think everyone in this office wants to jump your bones."

"Yes, well, I am going to be a senior art director. That does add to my sex appeal. However, since there is a strict agency rule against fraternization, consider yourself lucky that you didn't kiss me."

It was a silly rule, instituted in part because of a very messy affair the agency president, Rich Johnson, had had with a junior copywriter six years ago. As a condition of his second marriage—to the copywriter—his new wife insisted that employees involved in romantic relationships be subject to immediate termination.

But the agency regulations weren't all that was stopping them. She and Alex had developed their own set of guidelines, rules they'd both followed since that one night together. She hadn't allowed herself more than the occasional fantasy about her best friend since then. And any sexual tension that cropped up was laughed away.

She drew a deep breath. "Thank you for speaking up for me, Alex. I do appreciate it."

"No problem," Alex replied, his gaze capturing hers. They stared at each other for a long moment and Greta fought the temptation to reach out and run her fingers through his thick, dark hair. He was an impossibly handsome man. A woman would have to be blind not to see that.

When he wanted to, Alex Hansen could be sweet and thoughtful and funny, the best friend any girl could ever have. And though most people might consider their relationship a bit odd, Greta didn't care. He'd always been beside her, at the important moments, through the ups and downs of a string of not-so-great boyfriends… through an awful health scare when she found a lump in her breast…through the unexpected death of her father.

She couldn't imagine not having him around to depend upon. But the closer they both got to their thirtieth birthdays, the more Greta had to wonder about their future together. They wouldn't always be unattached. But who would be the first to find real love? With her track record, Greta suspected it would be Alex. And when the time came, she'd give him up, as gracefully as she could.

"Have I ever told you how much I love you?" Greta said. "In a purely platonic way?"

Alex chuckled. "Yes. You tell me all the time, Adler. You're the only woman who can say that to me without sending me running for the bathroom window."

"You've crawled out a bathroom window?"

"Twice," he said. "Remember my broken ankle? That wasn't from a pick-up basketball game."

"You lied to me?"

"I was ashamed. We have to have some secrets between us, Adler. I have a reputation to protect."

"I'm your best friend," she said. "We're supposed to tell each other everything."

"You didn't tell me about that time you thought you were pregnant," he said.

"How did you know about that?" Greta whispered, warmth creeping up her cheeks again.

"I saw the box for the test when I took out your garbage before your Super Bowl party. I figured if you wanted to tell me, you'd get around to it."

"Well, it was negative," she said, "so there was nothing to tell."

"So, we're agreed that, even if we are best friends, we don't have to tell each other everything, right?"

"Agreed," she said. It wasn't good to share everything. They couldn't be friends if one of them wanted to renegotiate the rules. Or if one of them was falling in love with the other. And it wasn't as if she was madly in love with him—she was just slightly confused right now and only occasionally attracted.

It was difficult to watch him blow through shallow relationships one after the other, to see him brush aside women who might be able to make him happy simply because of some silly flaw he detected. And yet, she was happy with each breakup, knowing that he'd be hers for just a little longer.

Greta knew that finding a man who would tolerate Alex's presence in her life had already created problems. Her last boyfriend had given her an ultimatum—"him or me"—and she'd chosen Alex.

"Complete honesty is overrated," she said.

"So you wouldn't want me to tell you your hair looks a little...poufy this morning."

"Poufy? How? What's poufy about it?"

He reached out and patted her on the top of her head. "I don't know. It's just sticking up kind of funny in the back. You might want to take a look in a mirror."

Greta glanced at her watch, then cursed softly. "I don't have time to fix it. They're going to be here any minute."

Alex sighed impatiently. "Just stand still and give me your brush." She retrieved it from her purse and Alex tugged it through her hair once or twice, then nodded. "All right. That looks better. It was just sticking up kind of funny. It made you look like a chicken."

"Thanks," Greta muttered, tucking her short-cropped hair behind her ears. There were some things she didn't like about their friendship. Sometimes he was too honest with her.

"If this goes well, we'll have to go out for drinks tonight," Greta said. "Very large appletinis. On you."

"Can't," he said. "I'm driving to Aspen for the weekend."

"Hot date?"

"No. No date, actually. Thea Michaels invited me and Dave MacDonald to use her mountain cabin this weekend. We were going to do some skiing, but Dave had to cancel." Alex paused. "Do you want to go?"

"The last time we skied together, I sat in the lodge and got drunk and you skied. I can't keep up with you on the black diamonds and you don't enjoy the bunny hill."

"Then you can…shop. Or sleep. Or work. Thea has a really nice place and she's been nagging me about it for months. She's my biggest client, so I figured I ought to accept her generous offer or risk pissing her off."

Greta had heard all about Thea Michaels and her divalike disposition. She'd demanded to choose her own creative team, then ignored all the talented women at the agency and surrounded herself with the young and attractive men on staff. Alex was Thea's account manager, and Dave, her art director.

"All right," Greta said. "I guess I could go." Except for their one-night stand, she and Alex had never spent twenty-four hours together, much less an entire weekend. At first, she wondered if their friendship could tolerate more than an eight-hour encounter. The last time they'd traveled to an auction in Colorado Springs, they'd gotten into a huge argument over sports in the car on the way home and hadn't spoken for a week after that.

"It'll be fun," he said. "Just don't insult my favorite hockey team and we'll get along just fine."

"As long as you don't go off on my taste in music, we won't have a problem."

"THIS IS A PROBLEM."

"We're almost there," Alex said. "And I'm used to driving in bad weather. You don't have to be so nervous. Relax. We'll get there when we get there."

"I'm not nervous," Greta snapped. "I just think we should have turned around and gone home once they decided to close the Denver airport."

"Where is your sense of adventure? It's a snowstorm, not the apocalypse. And if you grip the dashboard any tighter, your fingers are going to go gangrenous."

"You're doing this just to bug me, aren't you?"

"I'm doing this because tomorrow morning there's going to be fresh powder at Aspen and I have every intention of being the first one down the mountain."

"I think I might be having a stroke," Greta muttered. "My blood pressure has to be through the roof. If I start to slur my words, you need to turn around."

Alex chuckled to himself. That's the thing he loved about Greta. She had no filter and never tried to be anything but herself when they were together. Had he invited another girl for the weekend, she would have been acting exactly how she thought he wanted her to act, as if driving into a blizzard was an exciting adventure and not a calculated risk. And if she'd acted like Greta, he would have tossed her into the nearest snowbank. But Greta was Greta, his most annoying and adorable friend.

"Turn left, fifty yards," the GPS voice said.

"Turn left, fifty yards," Greta repeated.

Alex glanced at the GPS on the dash. "See. We're almost there. Just another mile down this next road and we'll—"

"What road?" Greta asked. "You can't even see the road we're on right now."

"I used my considerable powers of deduction, since there are trees on either side of this big white path through the forest."

"Turn right, twenty-five yards," the voice said.

"Turn right, twenty-five yards," Greta said. "This place better be worth it."

It should be. Hell, Thea had described the place in perfect detail and there wasn't a woman on the planet who would be disappointed—hot tub, steam shower, French bedding, a gourmet kitchen. Thea had even promised to stock the refrigerator with tempting selections. The moment they arrived, Alex planned to pour Greta a big glass of wine, draw her a hot bath and encourage her to relax after their six-hour drive.

An image flashed in his head at the thought of Greta in the bathtub. That would require her to get naked in very close proximity to him. It was an odd concept, he mused. Usually when women took their clothes off around him, hot sex followed.

He and Greta had enjoyed that pleasure only once in their seven-year friendship. The passion had been fueled by too many margaritas, Greta's recent breakup with the perfect boyfriend, and a two-month drought in Alex's sex life.

In all honesty, the sex had been really good, but Greta's hangover had been accompanied by a huge dose of remorse and very hazy memories of the event. He'd remembered every single moment. It had been wild and passionate and real…very real. Something he hadn't been able find with any other woman.

But Greta had wanted to forget that night and move on, so he'd agreed that in order to remain friends, they'd have to put their mutual indiscretion in the past. Still, the memory of her body, her perfect body, was seared indelibly into his brain. Even now, after a few years, he could still recall how she felt beneath his hands, how she tasted and how the desire between them had flamed out of control.

"Turn right, now," the GPS ordered.

"Turn right!" Greta said.

Alex squinted into the dizzying snow, searching for the turn. "Where? There's no road here." He'd been able to follow some earlier tire tracks on the main road, but there was nothing to indicate where he was supposed to turn. No sign, no tracks, just snow.

He slowed the car to a crawl. "I don't see it," he murmured. "Do you?"

"Maybe we missed it," Greta said.

"No, the GPS would have told us to turn around as soon as—"

"There," Greta said.

The road was narrow and covered in a deep blanket of snow. The Subaru wagon had done pretty well on the plowed surface earlier, but this side road hadn't been touched. "Shit," he muttered.

"Shit? What is that supposed to mean? We can't turn around now. We're six-tenths of a mile away from a warm bed. We are not turning around."

"I don't know if we can get through."

"I can't go for another three hours of this stress."

"I guess if we get stuck we can walk. I've got snow-shoes in the back and a flashlight in the glove box. We should be able to see the lights once we get close enough."

"I hope you brought a loaf of bread," Greta countered.

"There's food at the cabin."

"No, to leave a trail back to the car in case we get lost in the forest." She glanced over at him. "Hansen and Greta? Now all we need is a wicked witch and we'd be set for the weekend."

"This will be worth it," he said as he carefully turned onto the side road. "In a few minutes, you'll be safe in a warm mountain cabin. I'll even make you dinner."

"Damn right you will!"

They continued down the unplowed road, Alex watching the GPS as the tenths of a mile ticked by.

They were past a half mile when he felt the front wheels sink into a drift of snow. He pressed the accelerator, hoping the momentum would carry them through, but the increased speed brought on a swerve and in the blink of an eye, they slid off the side of the road.

Alex cursed. Even with the four-wheel drive on the Subaru, the drift was too deep. He could spend the next half hour shoveling, but they were so close to the cabin, it wasn't really worth it. They'd walk the rest of the way and he'd get the car out in the morning.

Right now, he needed to get Greta in front of a warm fire with the least amount of trouble as possible. He snapped the GPS out of its bracket and tucked it into his jacket pocket.

"Grab your bread crumbs, little girl. We're going to walk from here." He pointed to the glove box. "There's a flashlight in there. I'll get the snowshoes."

"We can't leave the car here," she said.

"It will be fine. I doubt that anyone will be out on the road tonight. But I'll call the sheriff's department and let them know where it is once we get to the cabin. I can shovel it out in the morning."

Alex pulled his hood over his head and ventured out into the snow. He kept most of his outdoor equipment in the back of the station wagon, always ready to take off for a fun weekend. He had a tent, two down sleeping bags, outdoor cooking equipment and freeze-dried food. If he and Greta were forced to rough it, they'd be warm and fed until the snow stopped.

He retrieved two sets of snowshoes from the back

and then helped Greta out of the car. "How are we going to carry our bags?" she asked.

"We'll leave them here," he said. "I'll come out later and get them."

"No, you're not coming out here alone, in the dark. I just need to grab a few things."

"I'll carry your bag," he said. "We'll leave mine here."

He grabbed the flashlight, then helped her fasten the snowshoes to her boots. Greta held the flashlight out in the swirling snow. "If I fall down on these things, I'm not going to be able to get up."

"I'll pick you up," he said. "We're not that far. And if the cabin isn't where it's supposed to be, we'll come back to the car and snuggle up for the night."

"Don't think you're going to seduce me like you do all your other women. I'm immune to your charms," she muttered. He turned the flashlight on her face and she managed a smile.

"You think I'm hot," he said. "I know it. I can see it in the way you look at me. Like you're undressing me with your eyes."

She reached out and slapped away the flashlight. "If you don't stop, I'm going to walk back to the nearest town and find a cheap motel. You are so full of yourself."

"All right, start out slowly. The shoes will feel a bit clumsy at first. Don't shuffle. Just pick up your feet and place them in front of you and you'll be fine."

He hoisted her bag over his shoulder, closed the car

door and took her hand. They hadn't taken more than ten steps before she got her feet tangled and pitched forward into the snow. Alex tried to catch her, but her bag shifted and he lost his own balance, coming down beside her.

He turned the flashlight on her as she sat up, her face covered with snow. Greta looked so ridiculous, he couldn't help but laugh. Reaching out, he brushed the snow from her cheek with his gloved hand.

"Stop!" she shouted. "This isn't funny. People die out here. They'll find our frozen bodies in the spring. We'll become a cautionary tale. Look at the two fools who drove into the middle of a blizzard for a free night at some dusty old cabin."

Alex gently brushed the snow from her hair, illuminating her features with the flashlight. "Do you want me to carry you?"

"I can walk," she said. "But I want to hold the flashlight."

Once on their feet, they started down the road again, guided by a narrow stream of light on the sparkling snow. The only sound breaking the silence of the forest was the gentle shush of their feet. There was no wind, and snowflakes silently drifted down on the chilly night air.

"Beautiful," he said.

"Lavishing me with compliments is not going to make me walk any faster," Greta said.

"I was commenting on the weather," he replied.

She stopped in her tracks and aimed the flashlight

into the dark forest. Alex prepared himself for another sharp comment, but then she took a deep breath and smiled. "Yes, it is really beautiful. It's so quiet. You can almost hear the snowflakes hitting the ground."

"I'm glad you decided to come along," he said. He reached out and took her hand, then dropped a friendly kiss on her forehead. "We're going to have lots of fun."

But as they walked toward the cabin, Alex found himself thinking of more than just fun. As he'd leaned over to kiss her, he'd almost made a detour to her lips. The impulse to really kiss her, full-on, lip-to-lip, with a little tongue, had been almost too much to resist.

Alex drew a deep breath of the cold night air. So what had changed? Did he want to alter the rules they'd made? Or was he just a little horny? Whatever it was, he had the whole weekend to figure it out.

THE CABIN APPEARED out of the snow like a golden beacon. Every light in the place was on and from a distance, it looked exactly like a snow globe, all hazy and picturesque.

As they walked closer, Greta saw that the place wasn't exactly what she'd consider a cabin. Though it was constructed of logs, their destination was more like a primitive-looking mansion. When they came close enough to the light spilling from the porch, she stopped and glanced over at Alex. His eyes were wide.

"Thea must have sent the caretaker up here to turn on the lights," he muttered.

"Why is she being so nice to you?" Greta asked. "I thought she was completely self-absorbed."

"She offered us a cabin for the weekend. I suppose she was trying to reward me and Dave for the work we've done."

"Yeah, I don't think that's it," Greta replied. "She's probably got some ulterior motive. And calling this a cabin is like calling the White House a cozy Colonial."

"Our ad campaigns have increased her business by thirty-seven percent over the past year. She's grateful. And after all the long hours I put in for her, I'm glad it's luxurious. Besides, what ulterior motives could she have?"

"She probably wants to get into your pants," Greta muttered. "After a weekend here, you're going to owe her."

"No!"

"You know, sometimes guys can be so dense," she said, shaking her head. "She's a cougar if I ever saw one. Just because she's over forty doesn't mean she can't be attracted to you. And she uses her power and her money to get exactly what she wants. Why do you think her whole team is young, sexy and male? What do men know about cosmetics? Let's face it, she likes the eye candy."

"She picked us for our talent," Alex said. "And she says that men are more inclined to see women as sexual objects, which is what she's trying to sell."

"She picked you because you have a pretty face and a hot bod."

"I should be insulted," Alex said. "But I promised myself we weren't going to fight this weekend."

The log structure was set into the mountainside, with walls of glass windows overlooking the rugged landscape. A covered porch circled two sides of the home and wide steps led up to the front doors.

Greta noticed an SUV parked in front, covered with snow. "I thought you said Dave couldn't come."

"He can't. His sister was coming to town."

"Someone is here," Greta said, pointing to the car. "Maybe he changed his mind."

Alex stopped dead in his tracks. "That's an Escalade. Thea drives an Escalade."

"Oh, well, there it is," Greta said with a satisfied laugh. "Adler scores. Game, set and match. I think we can finally agree on the motives behind this invitation."

"Maybe she came up to stock the cabin and got stuck in the snow," he said, continuing to the porch. "Or maybe she just wanted to get us settled before leaving for the weekend."

"Maybe she came for a ménage à trois," Greta suggested. "Dave plus Alex plus Thea does equal three by my count."

When they reached the front steps of the wide wraparound porch, Alex unhooked his snowshoes and stuck them into a snowbank. Then he helped Greta out of hers. They slowly walked up the steps.

"She said she'd leave the key on a hook under the porch swing."

Greta reached out and rang the doorbell, then stepped aside. "Why don't we try this first."

A moment later the door swung open and Thea Michaels appeared in all her splendor. She wore black silk lounging pajamas that were open in the front to reveal a lacy black bra. Her ash-blond hair was strategically mussed to look as if she'd just crawled out of bed and her lips were stained a luscious red. She just oozed sex appeal. Greta felt like a frump in comparison.

Alex drew a sharp breath and Greta smiled to herself. She wasn't often right, but when she was, it was pure pleasure. For a guy who prided himself on his intimate knowledge of women, Alex really was naive.

"Thea!" Alex said, stepping forward. "I didn't expect to find you here."

"Alex, darling. Come in, come in. You look like you trekked from the Arctic Circle. You're covered with snow." She looked at Greta. "Is that Dave?"

"No," Alex said as he stepped inside. "This is one of our art directors. Greta Adler. Dave couldn't come. He had a family obligation, so I invited Greta." Alex paused, then quickly draped his arm around Greta's shoulders. "She's my girlfriend."

Greta laughed out loud at his ridiculous statement, then covered her lips with her damp mitten. He might as well have said, "She's my pet raccoon" for all the conviction his words held. "Sorry," she murmured. "Cold air, dry throat."

To further prove his point, Alex pulled her closer.

"Greta, this is Thea Michaels, president and CEO of Te Adora Cosmetics."

Thea's expression slowly transformed from warm and welcoming to cool and aloof. "Your girlfriend?"

Greta swallowed another laugh and put on a calm expression. "I know. I can barely believe it myself. We just went official on Facebook yesterday," Greta explained. "It's so nice to meet you. Alex talks about you all the time."

"Strange. He's never mentioned you," Thea muttered, sending Greta a condescending glare.

"We always talk about business," Alex said. "I guess I misunderstood. I had no idea you meant this to be a business weekend."

"No, you were right. This weekend was supposed to be all about pleasure," Thea said. Her gaze was fixed on Alex and for a moment, Greta thought the woman was about to pounce. No wonder they called them cougars.

"Well, sixteen inches of new powder is about all the pleasure I can handle," Alex said. He glanced between them both. "Not that we don't enjoy…" He cleared his throat.

A long silence spun out between them. What was this woman waiting for? Greta wondered. She'd probably be thrilled if Greta just wandered out into the storm never to be seen again. It would serve Alex right! She knew what Thea Michaels had been up to all along. "Yes, we do enjoy that," Greta said. "But we wouldn't want to spoil your weekend. Maybe we should head back to Denver and—"

Thea sighed dramatically. "Don't be ridiculous. You'll spend the weekend, exactly as planned." She waved them inside. "Come out of the cold and take off your jackets."

Alex set Greta's bag on the floor, then gallantly helped her out of her jacket. He hung it in a nearby closet, before shrugging out of his parka. "This is a beautiful place," he said.

"I had it built a few years ago. I can be completely alone up here. I can walk around naked if I choose. Oh, and speaking of getting naked, there's a hot tub on the back deck and a whirlpool tub for two in the guest suite."

"All the comforts," Alex said.

"Yes. Well, let me show you to your rooms."

"Rooms?" Alex asked.

"Wouldn't you be more comfortable with separate rooms?" Thea cooed, reaching out and brushing snow out of Alex's hair. "We have plenty of bedrooms. No need to be crowded."

"That would be fabulous," Greta said. "He snores and sometimes I can't get a bit of sleep."

"No, one room is fine," Alex insisted.

"Top of the stairs," Thea said, irritation in her tone. "Why don't you two get settled and then join me for drinks." She wandered off in the direction of what Greta assumed was the kitchen, her hips swaying provocatively beneath the fabric of her pajamas.

"I love it when I'm right," Greta whispered.

2

"WE ARE NOT going to sleep in the same room," Greta insisted. "That point is not negotiable."

Alex tossed Greta's bag on the bed, then sat down, raking his hands through his damp hair. "I am not sleeping alone. If you're not in here with me, then she will be."

Greta paced in front of him, a worried expression on her pretty face. Alex grabbed her hand to stop her, forcing her to stand in front of him. "Just play along, Adler. I promise, I'll be the perfect gentleman."

"This place really is incredible," Greta said as she took in the luxurious interior of the bedroom. "I bet she brings all the men she wants to seduce up here."

Greta was right, Alex mused. This was no cabin, but a palace of seduction disguised as a mountain retreat. The lighting was designed for mood, the bedding made to appeal to the naked body, and the remote location perfect for any type of indoor or outdoor activity that required absolute privacy and discretion.

"I guess turning rotten pineapples into face cream has its advantages," Greta muttered, twisting out of his grasp. "It can buy you anything you want, including a man."

Alex cursed softly. "I don't want you making cracks about her business. She's still a client and I don't want anything that's said or done this weekend to mess that up."

Greta flopped down on the bed and threw her arms out. "Oh, please, just let me have a little fun with this. It will be the only bright spot of the weekend, I'm afraid."

Alex lay back beside her, then turned onto his stomach. "I'll admit it. You were right. Are you satisfied?" He could always trust Greta to get to the heart of the matter when it came to relationships.

"Did you see that outfit she was wearing? This was all a setup. Had you and Dave showed up, you would have been frolicking in the hot tub within an hour."

"I don't frolic with clients. Do you really think she planned to seduce both of us?"

"She probably just wanted Dave as a backup, in case you had a crisis of conscience."

"You really think she'd pick me over Dave?"

"Of course," Greta said. "You're much more attractive than Dave."

"He's taller," Alex said.

"Yes," Greta said. "But you have a much hotter body. And you're much prettier."

Alex groaned and buried his face in the down comforter. Then, he turned and looked at her. "She's attractive. I mean, there's no denying that Thea Michaels is hot. But she kind of scares me."

"You could stay in our room for the rest of the night. We'll pretend we're having sex." Greta got up on her knees and began to rock the bed. "Just groan every now and then. Oh, baby. Yes, baby. Just like that. Oh, more, more."

Alex reached out and grabbed her arm, pulling her back down. "Quiet, she'll hear you!"

Greta landed hard on his chest. Her eyes met his and for a moment, his breath froze in his chest as a sudden realization hit. He wanted to kiss her. Not just a platonic kiss, but a full-on meeting of the mouths. His gaze dropped to her lips.

Slowly, he slipped his fingers through the hair at her nape and drew her closer. His head began to spin and he took a quick breath, desperate for oxygen and the warmth of her mouth on his.

His senses had suddenly grown acute and he was certain she could hear his heart beating and the blood rushing through his veins. If he kissed her the way he wanted to, his life would change. He'd be forced to admit that he felt more than just friendship for her.

As he drew her closer, Greta closed her eyes, as if she welcomed what was coming. Would it feel as good as he remembered? All the rules they'd made to keep this from happening suddenly seemed ridiculously useless. It was just a kiss. One kiss. And when it was over, they'd go back to the way things were supposed to be between them.

"We shouldn't do this," he murmured, hoping for her approval rather than her agreement.

Greta opened her eyes. Alex watched her, seeing the expression on her face slowly change from expectation to resignation. "You're right," she said, the words dying in her throat.

He cursed softly and then shook his head, a smile twitching at the corners of his mouth. "No, I'm not."

Before she could draw another breath, his mouth came down on hers. They fell back onto the bed, the weight of his leg thrown over her thighs, his fingers still tangled in her hair.

Her mouth was warm, his tongue teasing hers until she surrendered completely. Desire coursed through his bloodstream, making his heart race. There had been a lot of women in his life since the last time they'd surrendered to their desire, but not one of them had been able to electrify his senses the way Greta did.

The kiss ended as quickly as it began. When Alex drew back, his common sense suddenly took control and he rolled off her, throwing his arm over his eyes. "I can't believe I did that. I'm sorry, Greta. I know we decided that—"

"No," Greta murmured. "If we're going to play a couple for your client, then I guess we have to get past any inhibitions we have about physical contact. It was just a kiss. It's not like we're going to go any further... right?"

He sat up and rubbed his face. "Right. I—I'm just

going to go downstairs and check on dinner plans. Why don't you get settled then join me."

Greta nodded as he pushed off the bed and headed to the door. "I really appreciate this, Adler. I'm not sure how to handle Thea, but it's much easier with you here."

When he reached the hallway, Alex closed the door behind him and leaned against it. This was the strangest position he'd ever found himself in. In the bedroom was a woman he wanted, one who didn't want him. And waiting downstairs was a woman who wanted him, one he didn't want at all.

He and Greta had settled the rules of their friendship a long time ago and the restrictions they put on any type of romance had served them well. But after that kiss, maybe it was time to renegotiate.

It had been a long time since he'd felt that kind of thrill kissing a woman. Lately, he'd begun to fear that he'd never find a woman who could make his pulse pound and his head spin. Still, Alex couldn't help wondering whether it was just the forbidden nature of the kiss that made it so powerful.

Breaking the rules had always been exciting to him. He'd lived his life jumping into new adventures without a thought to the consequences. On any other day, he might have even considered Thea's offer, if the conditions had been right and the risks minimal.

But something had shifted in the instant before that kiss, as if his inner compass had flipped upside down. North was south and south was north. He wanted Greta, not just for the night, but for…what? Forever? He already had that. They'd been friends for seven years, and they would remain that way as long as they followed the rules.

But he wanted to break the rules, to see what lay beyond friendship, to pick up where they'd left off after that drunken night four years ago.

Before he even attempted to seduce his best friend, he'd have to make sure everything was settled with Thea. Maybe this was all his fault. He'd been friendly to Thea and occasionally indulged in casual flirtation. But he couldn't recall ever saying anything she could have misconstrued. She was a mature and intelligent woman and knew the impropriety of getting involved with him. But unlike Greta, Thea Michaels didn't always play by the rules. If she saw something she wanted, she took it and damn the consequences.

And right now, Alex was pretty sure she wanted him—or maybe just an attractive male to warm her bed. He glanced back at the bedroom door, wondering what was going through Greta's mind.

Maybe he ought to go in and apologize. But he wasn't sorry about what had happened. How could he be? Kissing Adler, touching her, felt like the absolute right thing to do. He said a silent prayer, hoping that she felt the same way.

Alex slowly walked down the stairs. He found Thea standing in front of the fireplace, a glass of wine dangling from her perfectly manicured fingers, the silky fabric of her pajamas clinging to her well-toned body.

She slowly turned as she heard him approach. "Well, aren't we a cozy little threesome," she murmured.

"Is that what you were expecting when you invited Dave and me?" he asked, smiling weakly. "I have to give you credit, it was a bold move."

"I didn't get to where I am today by playing it safe," she murmured. "And just because you brought your little friend doesn't mean we can't enjoy ourselves. I can be discreet—if I have good reason. And you are definitely a good reason."

"Thea, as flattered as I am by the offer, I just don't think—"

"Oh, please, don't give me that excuse," she said, an irritated edge to her voice. "Surely you're bright enough to separate business from pleasure. I don't see any reason why we can't enjoy both sides of our relationship." She slowly strolled over to him and reached out to brush his hair from his forehead. "So, tell me about this girl. Is it serious or just a passing thing?"

"It's serious," he said, stepping away from her. The ease with which the words came out of his mouth caused him to pause. It wasn't a lie. He considered his friendship with Greta the most important in his life. "She's very…sweet."

"Bananas are sweet, but I wouldn't recommend a steady diet of them. Maybe you need hot."

"Thea, I appreciate—"

She pressed her finger over his lips. "We're both adults. We have needs. If you're worried about your job, Alex, I guarantee that nothing will change…except, of course, my affections for you. Which could actually work in your favor."

"Thea, I just don't think it would be a good idea. I'm…" He paused and swallowed hard. "I'm in love with Greta. Totally and completely in love. You are a beautiful, sexy and very tempting woman and under different circumstances, I would have jumped at the offer. But there are rules about these things. For good reason."

"And I thought you were the kind of man who enjoyed breaking the rules every now and then."

"You really don't know me outside our professional relationship."

"That's what this weekend was for," Thea replied. She took a slow sip of her wine, then set it down on a nearby table. "So how do they feel about your girlfriend at the office? Interoffice romance is usually not something management condones." She smiled lazily as she approached him again. "Unless no one knows. Are you keeping it all a secret, Alex? Because that would indicate to me that you *are* willing to bend the rules."

Alex gently took her hand from his shoulder then let it drop. "We haven't had dinner. And I'm starving. How about I make something for the three of us?"

"Forget dinner," she cooed.

"I'm hungry. And so is Ad—Greta. As long as we're all stuck here, we might as well enjoy a meal together."

"Fine. Let's start with a drink. You need to relax. What can I get you?"

"Beer?"

"Let me make you something guaranteed to relax you," she said. She wandered over to the wet bar near the kitchen and opened the liquor cabinet. Alex turned and found a safe spot near the fireplace where the wrought-iron tools would be close at hand if he needed a weapon to fend off an attack.

He shouldn't really be surprised that she was so persistent. Thea Michaels was a self-made multimillionaire, a woman who clawed her way to the top without the benefit of family money, business connections or higher education. And with that success came the ability to indulge in every little whim that crossed her mind.

Some of her romantic liaisons had been public relations disasters and her last affair, with an Argentinean polo player, had ended with her paying a hefty settlement to keep him quiet. It was no wonder she'd come looking in his direction. He was a safe bet, someone who'd have something to gain and lose from a dalliance.

But was his reputation really that bad? Around the office, he was known as a ladies' man and obviously Thea had decided to take advantage of his reputation. In the past, Adler had teased him about being a man whore, a skirt chaser and a slut puppy. He couldn't deny that he enjoyed the company of women. And he didn't feel the need to restrain himself.

But lately, he'd begun to tire of the game. Long nights trolling the bars, searching for someone who fascinated him, someone who held his interest longer than a drink or two. He and Adler had been spending more time together, painting her apartment, browsing antiques stores for furniture, ending a busy weekend with a Sunday-night movie and take-out Chinese.

In truth, he liked hanging out with Greta, better than any of his guy friends and certainly more than any woman he'd met in the past year. They had fun together, when they weren't bickering. And after what had passed upstairs, they shared a lot more than friendship.

Alex wasn't sure what the weekend held for him. It could be an unmitigated disaster or the beginning of something miraculous. As long as he kept his head on straight and avoided all the sexual land mines in the road, he'd survive.

But before he could make his escape, Thea caught his arm and pulled him to a stop. "I know what I want, darling," she said, running her fingers down his chest. "And if she doesn't please you, I'm sure I can."

"I'll keep that in mind." He forced a smile. "You know, I'm going to go check on Greta. I'm sure she's getting hungry by now."

"Such an attentive boyfriend," Thea murmured. "I hope she's worth it."

"Oh, she is," he murmured. And he was only just now beginning to realize just how much she meant to him.

GRETA SANK DOWN into the hot water, the bubbles washing up around her naked body. "Oh, this is bliss," she murmured, closing her eyes and allowing her mind to wander. French bubble bath, scented candles, plush cotton towels. This was exactly what she needed to wash away the stress and confusion of the day.

And yet, the moment she closed her eyes, Greta was plagued with memories of the kiss she and Alex had just shared. She ran her hands over her arms, surprised by the goose bumps that prickled her skin.

A knock sounded on the bathroom door and Greta sat up, crossing her arms over her breasts.

"Are you decent?" Alex called.

"I'm taking a bath," Greta replied.

He tried the door and found it unlocked, then walked in, his hand over his eyes. "All right, you need to get downstairs right now."

"Get out!" Greta cried, throwing a wet sponge at him. "I'm naked."

"I've seen it all before," Alex countered, parting his fingers to look at her. "What are you doing taking a bath? I need you downstairs to run interference."

"She's your client, you handle her."

He let his hand drop to his side. "That's exactly what she wants, to be handled." He crossed the room and sat down on the edge of the tub.

Greta sank back beneath the water, quickly scooping bubbles over her chest. She reached to grab more and watched as his gaze fixed on her breasts. Desire warmed her blood immediately and she stopped what she was doing, determined to taunt him for his intrusion.

Would she fight him if he reached out to touch her? Or would she melt into his arms, all soft flesh and damp skin? What if he stripped off his own clothes and climbed into the tub with her? Where would that lead?

Alex cursed beneath his breath. "Why are you taking a bath? You're not dirty. We haven't done anything all night long except sit in the car."

And make out on the bed, she added silently. "I'm tense. I need to relax."

"Well, come downstairs and drink a big glass of wine. I need your help."

"Why should I help you? You're the one who got us into this mess. If it wasn't snowing so hard, I'd make you take me home. But since we can't leave, I'm going to make the best of things. And this tub is a luxury I don't have at home. Look, I can stretch out."

He glanced down at her, his gaze running the length of her body. "I'm hungry," he murmured, his perusal stopping at the spot where the water met her breasts. "And I can't eat unless you're there."

"Why is that?"

"Because, if you're not there, I'm afraid I'm going to *be* dinner."

Greta sighed. "All right. Just give me a few minutes." She glanced over at him. "You can leave now."

"You sure you don't need help washing your back?"

She splashed water at him, hitting him on the face. In the moment she raised her arm, she knew she'd exposed her breasts to his view. But she didn't care. It served him right. Let him look.

Alex quickly stood and made a hasty retreat, closing

the door behind him. Greta grabbed a towel and stepped out of the tub. But a minute later, Alex stepped back inside again. He opened his mouth, as if to speak, then snapped it shut.

Greta stood beside the tub, her naked body gleaming in the candlelight, the towel clutched in her hand. For a long moment, neither one of them moved. Greta could hear her heart pounding in her chest and she waited for him to move, to speak.

"Did you want something else?" Greta finally asked, watching him with a wary gaze.

Alex cleared his throat. "I—I—" He shook his head. "Shit!" Clearly frustrated, Alex strode across the bathroom, cupped her face in his hands and kissed her.

His mouth covered hers in an urgent, almost frantic kiss and she melted against him. It was all she could think to do, operating solely on instinct. The towel fell out of her fingers as Alex's hands skimmed over her damp skin. When he reached her hips, he pulled her against him, his hands cupping her backside.

Greta felt the hard ridge of his erection beneath the fabric of his jeans. This hadn't been in her plan for the weekend. The last thing she'd ever intended was to allow him to seduce her again. But it felt so right, so perfect, as if every moment of the trip had been leading up to this.

When he finally drew back, Alex looked down at her. Greta's cheeks warmed and she caught a quick breath. Try as she might, she couldn't think of anything to say.

Alex reached down and grabbed the towel from the floor, then gently wrapped it around her body. "I'm just going to go now," he said, forcing a smile. "I—I'll see you downstairs."

The moment she was alone again, Greta sat down on the edge of the tub. She knew exactly where all this was leading. They'd been here once before, only the trip had been fueled by tequila and unresolved curiosity.

But this time was different. They were older and wiser and much better friends. She wasn't sure she had the will to stop it. As she toweled off, a tiny smile twitched at her lips. Maybe it was time to explore a few of her fantasies regarding Alex. If things had changed, it was a perfect way to find out how.

She wandered back out to the bedroom and picked through her bag for something comfortable to wear. First, she'd rescue him from Thea Michaels. Then, they'd retire for the evening. And after that…another shiver skittered over her naked body. Well, she'd just throw caution to the wind.

By the time Greta walked down the stairs, dinner had already been laid out on the table. Alex looked up at her as she approached, relief etched across his features. "There you are," he said, standing to pull out the chair next to him. He placed a clumsy kiss on her cheek and Greta pasted a smile on her face.

"Sorry," she murmured. "My bath was so relaxing I just couldn't bring myself to get out. I love those scented candles. I noticed they were part of your aromatherapy line, Ms. Michaels. They really work. I'm perfectly relaxed."

"Maybe we should force Alex into the bath," Thea said. "He's so tense."

"Let's eat!" Alex said, sitting down next to Greta. He reached out and handed her a bowl of Thai noodles. "Adler loves Thai food."

"You call her Adler?"

"Yes," Greta said, jumping in. "I refuse to let him call me any of those silly nicknames. Pookie, dumpling, sugarbun." She shuddered, wrinkling her nose for emphasis.

"Have some salad," Alex said, holding out another bowl.

"Men," Thea muttered, glancing back and forth between them both. "If they aren't thinking about sex, their minds are occupied with food."

"Lasagna," Alex said. "Darling, you love lasagna. And there's bread to go with it." She felt his hand on her thigh and he gave her a little squeeze, a silent plea. But for what? How far did he expect her to go in the charade?

"I love lasagna," Greta explained. "It's my favorite Italian food. We eat it all the time. At our favorite Italian restaurant."

"Gino's Trattoria," Alex said.

"Gino's," she repeated.

From the look on Thea's face, she wasn't buying the charade. Gathering her resolve, Greta leaned into Alex, snuggling up against him. "This really is wonderful. It's like a gourmet picnic."

Thea smiled seductively. "There are oysters. I ordered them especially for tonight. I've found in my experience that men who love raw oysters are very...oral. Do you like raw oysters, Alex?"

There was no doubting the meaning of her question. And the look in her eyes was enough to send a shiver down Greta's spine. She was like a cunning predator, waiting for just the right moment to pounce.

"Alex loves oysters," Greta said.

"Actually, I'm not big on raw seafood. It's just a case of food poisoning waiting to happen," he added.

The rest of the meal was like a sexual chess match—Thea on the offensive, Alex playing defense and Greta stuck in the middle trying to guess the next move before it happened. Though the food was good, she'd developed a nervous knot in her stomach that made even the most decadent tiramisu taste like cottage cheese.

She found herself thinking about indulging in another dip in the huge tub upstairs. Only this time, her fantasy included a tubmate. Her pulse leaped at the memory of feeling her naked body pressed against Alex's. That moment had been the single most arousing experience she'd ever shared with a man.

An excess of alcohol had blurred so much of their previous sexual encounter, but this instant had remained crystal clear in her mind. A shiver danced over her body and she drew a ragged breath.

Greta drained the last of her wine and set the glass

down in front of her. After two glasses, she should have been feeling a little tipsy, but her adrenaline had been pumping ever since she sat down at the dinner table and she felt completely clearheaded.

"That was a lovely meal," Greta said. "Thank you."

"I've never seen a woman eat with such…gusto," Thea said. "You really should be careful. Eating habits like that will catch up with you."

"Greta gets a lot of exercise. In fact, we always take a walk after dinner, don't we, darling?"

"A walk?" Greta asked, glancing over at Alex. "But it's cold and snowing and—"

"Come on," he said, standing up and grabbing her hand. "The fresh air will do you good. And I need to get my bag from the car. You're welcome to join us, Thea."

"You must be joking," Thea said, her voice dripping with condescension. "I never exercise unless my trainer is present. It's so much more efficient that way."

"Suit yourself," Alex said with a shrug. He quickly pushed back his chair and pulled Greta along to the front door. "Well, we'll be back soon."

"A walk?" she whispered to him as she pulled on her boots. "In the middle of a snowstorm? Couldn't you think of some other way to get away from her?"

"Do you have any suggestions?"

"No. But it's cold outside and I don't want to go out into the cold. I—"

"Just put your jacket on," he said. Alex helped her

into her gloves and pulled her hood up around her face, then leaned over and dropped a kiss on her lips.

"What was that for?" she asked.

"Just playing the part," he replied with a smile.

3

THEY STEPPED OUT onto the snowy porch and shut the door behind them. Greta took a deep breath and closed her eyes, leaning back against the log wall of the house.

"Are you all right?" Alex murmured, his gaze scanning her face for a clue to her thoughts. She'd played her part well. But just how far was she willing to go to protect him?

"Fine," she whispered. "Just exhausted from the stress of sitting at a table with Thea Michaels." She opened her eyes. "Let's just walk back to the car and drive home. Please? I don't want to spend the night here. I want to sleep in my own bed."

"It'll take me an hour to dig us out. And the roads are going to be impossible. They won't plow until it stops snowing. And it will be worse than it was on our way here." Alex reached out and slipped his arms around her waist. "Don't let her bother you. Once we go to bed, we won't have to deal with her until the morning."

"She called me fat," Greta cried.

"Shh! She can probably hear us inside."

"Not unless she has her ear against the door," Greta said. "And if she does, I'd just like to say that she has some pretty chunky thighs herself."

Alex took her hand and led her to the far end of the porch. "When did she call you fat? I didn't hear her say it."

"She said I ate with gusto. I hate her. She is such a witch. If there were an oven in that house big enough for her, I'd toss her inside."

"You'd put her in the oven?"

"Like the witch in 'Hansel and Gretel.' God, haven't you been paying attention?" She brushed a strand of hair out of her eyes and stared up at him. "I don't care how long it takes to get home. I promise, I won't complain about your driving. I'll just sit quietly."

"For you, that would be impossible. We'll just say we're tired and go to bed. Then, we'll get up early tomorrow morning and leave. I promise."

Was she really so averse to spending the night under the same roof as Thea Michaels? "Is it Thea you're worried about?" Alex asked, not really wanting to hear the answer. "Or is it me?"

Greta's breath clouded in front of her face as she sighed softly. "Why would it be you?"

"Well, I thought maybe after what happened in the bathroom you might—"

"No," Greta said.

"No? What does that mean?"

She drew a deep breath and sighed. "I don't know. I—I guess I'm just trying to play the part."

"Is that all it is?"

"What else would it be?" Greta asked.

"Well, you're doing a fine job," Alex said. "Except for that crack about the oysters."

"You like oysters. I figured the closer we keep to the truth, the easier it would be. Although, Thea was right about you being very oral. You just can't seem to keep from putting your big foot in your mouth."

Alex chuckled. "Quiet. She'll hear you."

"She's quite the creature, isn't she? Claws like a cougar, teeth like a barracuda and ears like a bat. I wonder if she has sex like a rabbit?"

"Stop," Alex said, holding up his hand. "I don't need that image burned in my brain for the rest of the evening." He gave her a quick hug. "Thanks for running interference."

"That's me. Your very own sexual linebacker. What would have happened if I hadn't been here?" Greta asked. "Would you have slept with her?"

He shook his head. "No."

"Really?"

"No! She's a client. I don't mix business with pleasure."

"We mixed business with pleasure when we slept together," Greta said. "And when you kissed me on the bed. And in the bathroom."

"I don't think of it that way," Alex replied. "I don't

think of you as a coworker. Come on, Adler, you're my best friend."

"But what does that mean? If you had to choose between me and your job, which would you choose?"

"That's simple. I can always find another job, but I'll never find another friend like you."

Greta searched his face, a wary expression suffusing her pretty features. "You're just saying that so I keep playing your girlfriend," she said.

He shook his head. "No, I'm saying it because it's true. I do care about you, Adler."

Greta stared up at him, her mouth agape. She began to speak, but then thought better of it. Alex waited for the tirade, a recap of all the rules followed by a warning that there wouldn't be a repeat of their previous indiscretions. Instead, to his surprise, she threw her arms around his neck and kissed him.

At first, her move startled him and he drew back. But then, an instant later, he decided to take advantage of this surprising event. Alex's lips covered hers in a long, lingering kiss. Greta moaned softly as he pressed her back against the log wall, his hands braced on either side of her head.

This was becoming a habit between them. So much that it almost felt natural to lose himself in the taste of her mouth. His gloved hands drew her closer, but their thick jackets created a barrier between them. He reached and unzipped her coat, smoothing his hands around her waist and pulling her toward him.

All around them, the snow continued to fall silently,

illuminated by the light spilling from the house. But Alex didn't notice the cold. His heart was pounding. In truth, he wanted to tear off all her clothes and take complete control of her beautiful body.

A shiver shook her and Alex drew back to look down into her eyes. "It's cold out here," he said. "Go back inside. I'll get my things and be back before you know it."

"She's going to eat me for dessert," Greta said.

"Just go inside and lock yourself in our room. I promise I'll be back to protect you in ten minutes."

"I—I thought I was the one protecting you," Greta said.

"And you've done a fine job of it, Adler. Now, go upstairs and get ready for bed."

Greta nodded and turned for the door. But then she glanced over her shoulder at Alex, her curiosity getting the better of her. "Would you step in front of a bus to save my life?" she asked.

He chuckled. "In a heartbeat."

Satisfied, she opened the front door and stepped inside. His decision had been made. Whatever happened tonight between them would be no cause for regret. Every time they touched, it was proof that she wanted more, that she was ready to experience the ultimate intimacy with him, to lie naked in his arms, to touch his body at will.

For this one night, maybe they could throw away all the rules. He walked down the front steps and grabbed his snowshoes, then strapped them on his feet. As he hiked back to the road, Alex pushed his pace, determined to get back to Greta as quickly as possible.

The road still wasn't plowed, but he found the car quickly, opened the hatch and grabbed his bag. Unzipping it, he rummaged through the contents then breathed a sigh of relief when he found the box of condoms. At least he'd be prepared for any eventuality.

But he realized that he wasn't ready to make that decision—not yet. Tossing his bag back inside, he grabbed the shovel he kept in the back of the car and set to work on the drift that had trapped the front wheels. The hard work was enough to rid him of some of his nervous energy and after just fifteen minutes, he'd managed to free the car and drive it back down to the cabin.

When he finally climbed the front steps, he was covered with snow and cold to the bone. The exercise had done the trick though. He felt pleasantly exhausted and relaxed. And though he still had sex on the brain, at least he had a shot at falling asleep with Greta sharing his bed. But as he reached for the door, he wondered if he'd have to get through another round with Thea before he could join Greta in the bedroom.

He didn't want to be rude, but if she insisted on this pursuit, he wouldn't have much choice. Why was she so intent on bedding him? Was it just the conquest? Alex couldn't imagine that she was interested in anything more than just sex. Though he'd heard Thea often invited men into her bed, she rarely allowed them a place in her life.

Drawing a deep breath, he stepped inside the cabin.

The interior was dimly lit and silent. A fire still crackled in the stone fireplace and he saw Thea, lounging on the sofa, another drink in her hand.

Alex slipped out of his boots and jacket, then crossed the room. "I thought you'd be in bed by now," he said.

"It's eleven o'clock," she said. "Children go to bed at this time. By the way, your girlfriend has already turned in." She patted the place beside her on the sofa. "Sit. Relax. Let me get you a drink."

"I'm fine," Alex said. He took another deep breath and tried to frame his words as carefully as possible. "Thea, I want you to know that in another time and another place, this may have happened. You are an incredibly sexy woman. But, I'm pretty sure the two of us, together, would be a disaster. We have a great professional relationship and I love working for you. I want to keep it that way. So, I'm going to have to say no to your very interesting proposition."

"What a pity," Thea said. "We would have had some fun together, Alex."

"Yes," he said. "I suspect we would have had lots of fun." He leaned over and kissed her cheek. "Good night, Thea."

She sighed softly, then shrugged. "Good night, Alex."

He strode to the stairs and climbed to the second floor. Alex wasn't sure what his decision might cost him professionally, but at the moment, he really didn't care. His thoughts were completely focused on the woman waiting for him in his bedroom. He'd managed to convince Thea he didn't want to sleep with her. Now he'd have to convince Greta of the exact opposite.

GRETA SAT IN the center of the bed, the sheet pulled up around her naked body. She reached over to turn on the light, then thought better of it. What was taking him so long? Had Alex decided to spend a little more time with Thea? She groaned softly. Oh, God, what if she was seducing him right now?

She flipped off the light. Maybe it would be easier if she didn't have to look at his face when he walked in. She flipped it back on. No, it would be best to see his reaction from the start. If it didn't look good, she might be able to spare herself a small measure of humiliation. She reached for her T-shirt at the end of the bed, then tossed it aside.

"No," she murmured. She wasn't fooling herself. She was reading all the signs right. He wanted her as much as she wanted him. But how far would he allow it to go before he called an end to it?

She flopped back on the bed and pulled the pillow up over her face. She knew Alex better than any other man on the planet, sometimes better than he knew himself. And what was happening to them, all these feelings and passions, they couldn't be ignored. They had two choices—continue to fight this attraction or appease their desire and then carry on with their friendship.

They'd done it once before. Maybe this was all they needed to maintain their friendship—sex every four years. But then again, maybe sex this time would ruin everything. The thought of never talking to Alex again, never being able to count on him, caused a deep ache in her heart.

Greta heard the door open and she froze, the pillow still over her face. What now? She'd told herself she'd decide by the time he returned and here he was. She heard the click of the lamp and bit back a moan.

"Adler?" he whispered. "Are you asleep?"

"Yes," she mumbled into the pillow.

"If you're asleep, why are you talking?"

She slowly pulled the pillow away and looked at him.

Alex grinned, his hands shoved in the back pockets of his jeans. "Are you naked under there?"

"Yes," she said. "Where have you been?"

"I dug the car out. Didn't you bring anything to sleep in?"

"Yes," she said. "I thought you and Thea might be…"

"Not a chance." He paused. "So, you're naked because…"

"Don't make me say it," Greta replied. She reached out and drew back the covers on the opposite side of the bed. "Just take your clothes off and get in."

He stared at her in disbelief. "What's going on, Greta?"

He rarely called her Greta. And at this moment, her name on his lips sounded so intimate, so serious. "I figure, every four years we get this…itch. Rather than suffer through all the silliness, it makes sense just to sleep together. And this is as good a time as any, don't you think. We're actually killing two birds with one stone."

"Are you sure?" he asked, setting his bag on the floor next to the bed. "You're not drunk, are you?"

"No," she said. "What difference would that make?"

"Technically, it hasn't been four years since the last time."

"Do you really want to nitpick right now? Because if you do, you can sleep with Thea."

Alex sat down on the edge of the bed and met her uneasy gaze. "I told myself after the last time that if we ever decided to give it another shot, I'd make sure neither of us were drunk. I just didn't expect your suggestion would sound so…"

"So what?" she retorted. "Desperate?"

"No, practical."

"Are you in or are you out?" she asked.

Greta watched as he tugged his sweater over his head and tossed it aside. His T-shirt followed, revealing a smooth expanse of muscular chest. When he stood and reached for the button on his jeans, she drew a sharp breath and he paused.

"Too fast?" he asked.

"Yes," she murmured. "Can you slow down? Just a little bit?"

He nodded, smiling at her the whole time. Alex slid across the bed, stretching out beside her, the bedcovers the only thing between their bodies. "So maybe you should tell me what we're going to do after I take my jeans off. Just so I'm prepared."

"Was Thea still downstairs when you came in?"

He nodded. "I think she was waiting for me," Alex said.

"Did she try to kiss you?" Greta asked.

"No," Alex said. "But I kissed her. On the cheek."

His admission didn't make her feel any better. In truth, talking about Thea was just a way to waste a little time until she was ready to touch him. Once she did, there would be no going back.

"I don't want Thea," he whispered, smoothing his palm over her cheek.

A long silence grew between them. "Do you want me?" Greta asked.

Alex slowly nodded. He leaned closer and brushed his lips against hers. "I want you, Greta. I've wanted you for a long time, I think, but I've managed to convince myself otherwise. But now, I think maybe we should stop pretending to be best friends and start believing that we might be something more."

Greta sat up, wrapping the sheet around her bare breasts. "No! That's not how it should be."

"Are you saying that you've never thought about us… together? Because I think you'd be lying. We've both considered the possibility, a hundred times over. And we've both been too scared to do anything about it. But maybe it's time we did."

"Romance will ruin our friendship," she said. "But sex won't. We survived having sex once before. We can do it again."

"I think friendship might make a romance work. I've

never been friends with a woman before. Maybe that's
what's been missing."

Greta scanned his face, looking for some assurance
that he truly meant what he was saying. Was he really
suggesting they try to be more than friends? She'd allowed herself a few romantic fantasies about Alex, but
she'd been quick to push them aside. Usually, when she
allowed herself to daydream about him, it was purely
sexual. Sex could be simple between them, but love was
a whole different story. "How long have you felt this
way?"

"For a while. Although I think I've been trying my
best to ignore the feelings."

"How? By dating every big-boobed blonde in the
city of Denver?"

"They were distracting," he said with a smile. "But
they weren't you."

"And what if there's nothing between us? No spark.
No chemistry."

"Then we know we're friends and nothing more.
Wouldn't you much rather know for sure than live with
all this doubt?"

It sounded good. But she wasn't all that sure that
she wanted to know. Maybe the reason she'd been so
determined to maintain their friendship was because,
deep down, in a secret corner of her heart, she'd always
hoped that someday he'd choose her. That she'd be his
one and only.

But she'd never allowed herself to really consider
the possibility. Greta knew that if they tried being more

than friends and it didn't work, she'd never be able to go back to their former relationship. She'd become just another in a long line of discarded women, good enough to warm his bed for a few weeks and nothing more.

What was going on in his head? Where did he think this night might lead? "Are you sure this isn't about making a good show for Thea?" she asked.

Alex shook his head. "You know, a few years ago, I might have slept with her. But now, I know how disappointed that would have made you. You make me a better man, Adler. And I think maybe it's time you benefitted from all your hard work."

His revelation stunned her. In truth, she assumed he really didn't listen to any of her nagging. She'd tried to convince him to be the kind of man she'd always imagined as perfect. And now, he was offering himself to her. How could she refuse?

"All right," she said softly. "But if either one of us decides this isn't working, then we go back to being friends. You have to promise me that." It might be an empty promise, but Greta needed his assurance either way.

He stared into her eyes. "If that's the way you want it, I promise. We'll always be friends."

Greta drew a deep breath. "All right. I just need a moment." She grabbed her T-shirt from the end of the bed and tugged it over her head, then slipped out from beneath the covers. "I'll be right back."

Alex rolled over on his back. "I'll be waiting."

Greta hurried to the bathroom and closed the door

behind her. She flipped on the light, then stood over the sink, staring into the mirror.

"This will change everything," she murmured to her reflection. And though she wanted to believe they could go back, in her heart, she knew it wasn't likely. Was it worth the risk?

ALEX GLANCED OVER at the bathroom door. Greta had been locked inside for the past five minutes. Though he could imagine what she might be doing, as the seconds ticked by he began to realize that maybe she wasn't ready for this.

He knew her so well. She'd be running over all the pros and cons, making a mental list of the possible consequences and weighing each carefully. Hell, it took her fifteen minutes to decide which laundry detergent to buy. Considering the ramifications of this night, she might be in the bathroom until dawn.

Over time, he'd begun to wonder if her indecisiveness with men was because her standards were too high. Then he wondered if she was carrying a secret torch for him. Alex didn't like to imagine she was in love with him. He'd often wondered if that was why he spent so much time pursuing other women—he was afraid of failing with Greta.

Hell, he didn't have a clue why he'd done what he'd done in the past. But tonight, for the first time in his life, he knew exactly what he wanted and why. And he needed to believe that Greta was just as certain as he was.

With a groan, he rolled off the bed and crossed to the bathroom door. Alex decided not to bother knocking. He opened the door to find her sitting on the edge of the whirlpool tub, her hands clutched in front of her. She looked so pathetic that he couldn't help smiling. Without a word, he moved to take her hands and pull her to her feet. His mouth came down on hers, softly teasing until she surrendered to the kiss.

Her body went soft in his arms and Alex smoothed his hands over her back until they rested on her hips. She wasn't wearing anything beneath the T-shirt and the temptation to touch naked skin was overwhelming. But he knew she'd have to take the lead.

"Are we really going to do this?" she whispered.

"That is entirely up to you," he replied. Alex grabbed her hand, then pressed his lips to her wrist, toying with her fingers as he did. "I think it's time we figure out what's going on between us," he said.

"We're friends."

"Come on, Greta. We both know it's more than that. Only we've been too afraid to admit it."

"What if this ruins everything?" she asked.

"And what if it makes it even better?" he countered. He saw the surrender in her eyes and he felt a current of fear pass through him. He wanted it to be good. No, not just good. Amazing. "So, how do you want to start?"

"I don't know." Greta closed her eyes and shook her head. "I'm sorry. I'm really, really nervous."

"We're friends. It can't be that hard. And we have done it before. Why don't you start by touching me."

"Or maybe you could touch me," Greta said.

"I could," Alex murmured, sliding his palm along her hip and beneath her shirt. He slipped his other hand around her nape, weaving his fingers through her hair and drawing her nearer. "How's this?"

Spinning her around, he pressed her back against the edge of the marble-topped sinks, his mouth searching for another taste. This time, she reacted, her fingers splaying over his chest as the heat between them grew.

He knew her so well, all her silly quirks and stubborn beliefs. But Alex didn't know this part of her, the woman beneath his best friend. For so long, he'd considered her just another girl. But that had suddenly changed.

As her hands smoothed over his shoulders, he felt a tremor of need rock his body. He wanted her, but not just in a physical sense. They'd shared so much that it felt only right to share this too. And this time, he'd remember every single moment of it.

Alex picked her up and wrapped her legs around his waist, then carried her back to the bedroom. They tumbled onto the bed, rolling together until they found a comfortable spot. He kissed her again, surprised at how natural it suddenly felt.

This wasn't the stubborn, opinionated, bossy friend he'd always known. Greta was soft and vulnerable, her body pliant beneath his touch.

When she reached for the button on his jeans, Alex knew she'd made her decision. If she had any doubts, they were gone now. He rolled onto his back and watched as she worked at his fly with nervous fingers. Reaching out, he brushed the hair from her eyes and smiled at her. When his zipper was undone, he slid his jeans over his hips and kicked them off onto the floor.

His desire was evident through the thin cotton of his boxers and Alex worried that she might think this was just about sex. He wanted to tell her how he felt, how it didn't matter if they went that far. This was about getting closer, even closer than they already were.

Greta lay down next to him, wrapping her arm around his waist and tucking her body into the curve of his arm. "What are you thinking?" he murmured.

"Nothing."

"You're always thinking about something, Greta. I know you too well. That brain of yours never stops working."

She sat up, tucking her feet beneath her backside, and watched him warily. Then she placed her hand on his chest and slowly smoothed her fingers down to his belly. The sensation caused his breath to catch in his throat. "That's what I was thinking," she said.

"What?"

"I was wondering if I could make you feel the way all those other women did."

Alex gasped. How could she even think of comparing herself to them? Besides the females in his family, Greta was the most important woman in his life. "None of those other women have what you have. Why do you think they never lasted? Because I was always comparing them to you."

"You were?"

"Yeah. I think I was. I didn't really realize it until now, but I could never be completely honest with them. Not like I am with you."

"I feel the same way," she said.

"Then I think you should kiss me now and start thinking about you and me."

She laughed softly. "All right. I guess I can do that."

Alex grabbed her around the waist and pulled her on top of him. His hands cupped her naked backside as he drew her into another kiss. But this time, the kiss did what it was meant to do. Slowly, all her hesitation dissolved and she left her insecurities behind.

Before long, it wasn't enough just to feel each other through the barrier of the clothes they still wore. Only skin-to-skin contact would satisfy. He tugged at her T-shirt, pulling it over her head and tossing it aside. His boxers followed and when they were finally naked, Alex was free to focus on enjoying her body.

Though Greta was usually so dismissive of her physical beauty, Alex saw perfection. She wasn't enhanced by artificial means, just natural. From her hair to her nails to her breasts. Everything was as it should be.

He moved to kiss her breast, then teased at her nipple with his tongue. It grew to a hard peak and he moved to the other, all the while listening to the soft moans coming from deep inside her. Her fingers tangled in his hair and she pulled him back into a kiss.

They had all the time in the world and yet they seemed to be in a rush to find out where all their hidden desire would lead. He held his breath as Greta's caress found more intimate territory. And when she wrapped her fingers around his hard shaft, a shudder ran through him.

Moments of intense pleasure spun out around them. This wasn't so much a seduction as it was a discovery, like uncovering a hidden treasure that had been right in front of them all the time.

Why had it taken so long for him to realize how he really felt about Greta? Had some instinct warned him off until now? Had the planets finally come into alignment? Maybe destiny did have a hand in this after all.

Greta trailed a line of kisses across his collarbone, then drifted lower, to his chest and then his belly. Alex held his breath, knowing what was coming, certain it would send him over the edge. Her tongue lingered at the tip of his shaft before she took him into the warm recesses of her mouth.

Alex's mind flashed to an image of Greta with all the boyfriends who'd passed through her life. Had she pleased them in this same way? Jealousy surged through him along with waves of pleasure. From this point on, there would be no others. Greta belonged to him.

To prove his point, he grabbed her hands and pulled her up along his body. He'd tucked a box of condoms beneath the pillow while she was in the bathroom and he retrieved them now, handing them to her. "I think we need these," he murmured, his gaze fixed on her flushed face.

"I think we do," she whispered, a smile touching the corners of her mouth. She removed one from the box and opened the package, then gently sheathed him.

Alex had done this so many times, he knew exactly what was about to happen. But as she sank down on top of him, her knees on either side of his hips, he felt as if it was his first time. His senses had been heightened, his nerves alert, so every single movement sent frissons of pleasure pulsing through his body.

There was nothing he could do to stop himself. Instinct took over and he rolled her beneath him, dragging her knees up around his waist. She moaned softly, running her fingers through his hair as he pressed his lips to her neck.

Over the years, there were moments when he felt so close to Greta. But this was something different. They were both sober and acutely aware of the risk they were taking. And yet, it all seemed so right, so natural.

Alex kissed her again and she arched against him, her breath coming in shallow gasps as his rhythm quickened and his need built. The instant he felt her dissolve into her release, Alex was there, following her over the edge.

Wave after wave of exquisite pleasure washed over him and when it was finally over, he held her face between his palms and kissed her deeply. There were no words, only the silent understanding that this would not be the last time.

4

"IF YOU SPEND any more time in that tub, you're going to start looking like a prune," Alex said, standing in the doorway of the bathroom.

Greta opened her eyes and looked over at him. A tiny thrill raced through her at his rumpled appearance. She'd been the cause of the mussed hair and the love bite on his neck and the sleepy look in his eyes.

He wore just his jeans, low on his hips, the top button undone, and a satisfied smile on his lips. They'd been so incredibly good together last night, better than she'd ever imagined in all her unbidden fantasies.

Their first time together had been so frantic, over before either one of them realized what they were doing. Regret had set in immediately, cooling the lust like a blast of Arctic air. But last night, they'd savored each sensation, taking their time to explore new experiences together before moving on.

"I didn't hear you get up," he said.

"You were dead to the world, so I figured I'd let you

sleep. I think Thea is gone. Her car isn't parked out front anymore."

She smiled. "We're all alone."

He sauntered over to the tub. "Good," he said. "I've got you exactly where I want you. All wet and naked." Alex knelt down next to the tub, then kissed her shoulder. "She must have left the minute the plow came through."

Greta straightened. "I'm surprised. I thought she was more determined than that to get you into bed."

"Maybe she heard us last night and decided it was a lost cause?"

Greta gasped. "We weren't that noisy." She paused. "Were we?"

Alex chuckled. "Maybe just a little. I didn't expect that. I mean, I've known you for years and I've never seen that side of you before. Never suspected it was… there."

"Did you assume I was some kind of prude?"

"I just didn't remember it being that way the first time we did it. It was good then, don't get me wrong, but last night was…wow. Surprising, I guess."

"We were both pretty drunk that first time," Greta said. "I'm not sure we would have done anything if we'd been sober."

"Do you regret what happened?" Alex asked. "Not then, but last night, I mean."

Greta shook her head. "No. I've always wondered what it might be like, given a second try at it…and a third and fourth. A chance to do it right."

He grinned and picked up a sponge from a basket next to the tub and dipped it in the water, then slowly began to wash her back. Greta sighed, pure contentment overwhelming her. This was how it was supposed to be, she mused. This was the way she'd always imagined a relationship with a man to feel like—comfortable, intimate, easy. Why couldn't she have found this for herself?

She'd dated lots of men, been intimate with some of them as well, but with Alex, it all seemed right, as if they…fit. Was it because they were such good friends? Or maybe it was because this was only meant to be a one-night stand. There were no expectations beyond the walls of this room to confuse them both.

Greta silently chided herself. They'd made an agreement. In fact, she'd insisted on it. Just one night. If either of them was unhappy, that was it. Once they left the cabin, they'd go back to life as it was before. They'd be best friends. She drew a shaky breath, pinching her eyes closed. Could she do it? Could she ever look at Alex again and not see the naked man moving above her? Could she ever crawl into bed and not think of his hands on her body.

"I love this bathtub," she murmured, determined to occupy her mind with idle conversation instead. "I don't have a tub in my apartment and I never realized what a luxury it is to just sit, surrounded by hot water. I think I'd come home from work every day and have a bath."

Alex slid the sponge down to the small of her back.

"I have a big tub at my place. You're always welcome to come over and use it."

"Mmm," she said, leaning forward. "Be careful what you wish for. With your social life, I'm not sure you'd appreciate a naked woman turning up in your tub unexpectedly."

"I don't think I'd mind so much," he said softly. "Especially if that naked woman was you."

A shiver skittered over her arms, raising goose bumps. Was he just teasing, too? Or did he really mean what he said? Greta wondered. Was he thinking that this might continue, that there was something more than just a one-night stand between them?

There it was again. Expectations. They always ruined the best of friendships. That's what made Alex and Greta work so well. They never demanded anything of each other—except honesty. And loyalty. And complete and utter trust.

But wasn't that what made all the great romances work, as well. That and undeniable passion. After last night, they had that one down perfectly. When she thought about it, she and Alex had all the things she was looking for in a romantic relationship—except the romance.

"A tub like this really isn't practical," Greta murmured. "I mean, it's impossible to wash my hair."

"Sure you can," Alex said. "That's what that sprayer thing is for." He reached out and picked up the hand spray from the bracket at the end of the tub.

"That just gets water all over the bathroom," Greta said.

"No, it doesn't," he countered. "You just have to be careful. Here, I'll show you."

"No!" Greta replied. "I don't want to wash my hair now, I was just commenting that it—"

"I'll wash your hair for you and then you can—"

"I don't want my—" Greta stopped herself. If she had any worries that things had changed between them, she could put them aside. They'd gone right back to bickering at the first available opportunity. "All right," she said. "Show me how it works."

"It would work a lot better if I got in the tub with you," he suggested.

Greta drew a quick breath, hearing the desire beneath his practical suggestion. "Sure."

Grinning, Alex stood and skimmed off his jeans. He was already getting hard and Greta took the opportunity to catch a glimpse of his body. He didn't do much for exercise except run a few times a week. Alex's body hadn't been toned in the gym. Instead, he spent his time in constant movement skiing, biking, skating. If it could be done outdoors, Alex found time to do it. Added to the calories burned in the bedroom, it was no wonder he looked so good.

He sank into the water, sitting opposite her, sighing softly as he settled himself in the tub. "This is nice. But it would probably work better if you turned around." He grabbed her waist and before she knew it, Greta was sitting between his legs, her back resting against his chest.

She felt her pulse quicken as his erection pressed against the small of her back. Why bother with her hair? Why not just forget the silly foreplay and get down to business. They only had a day to rid themselves of all the simmering desire. And the only way to do that was to indulge in a few more really good orgasms.

"Tip your head back." He turned on the sprayer and warm water sluiced through her hair. A moment later, the scent of almonds filled the air as he began to work the shampoo through the wet strands.

Oh, she could really get used to this, Greta mused. It was the ultimate luxury and she felt her body relax as he gently massaged her scalp. "You're good at this," she said. "You must have had a lot of practice." The moment the words were out of her mouth, she wanted to take them back. But she couldn't help feeling a bit jealous of all the other women who'd come before her.

"Nope. I've never washed a woman's hair before," Alex said. "But how hard could it be? The instructions are on the bottle. Lather, rinse, repeat."

"No repeat," Greta said. "I don't repeat."

"Good to know," Alex murmured. "I'll remember that for next time."

As he rinsed the soap from her hair, he slipped his arm around her waist and cupped her breast in his palm, teasing at her nipple with his thumb. She sank back against him, losing herself in the sensation.

Greta tried to imagine them in a real relationship. Would they ever leave the bedroom or would every waking hour be spent in passionate pursuits? An image of the two of them tearing at each other's clothes in Alex's office flashed in her head.

"I can't get enough of you," he murmured. "It's strange."

"It is?"

"I've seen you at work every day for the past seven years, but I never really saw you like this. Naked and soft…and willing."

He slid his palms over her belly, dipping beneath the water and sending tingles of anticipation up and down her spine. It hadn't taken him long to learn what made her ache with need. His fingers found the spot between her legs and Greta moaned.

Why was it so simple to give in to him? Was it the trust they shared as friends? Alex was the only man she knew who would never intentionally hurt her. Doubt pierced her hazy thoughts. Was she sure of that? He'd walked away from a long string of lovers without a second thought. What made her think she would be any different?

She wouldn't be, Greta thought to herself. And she could accept that as long as they remained friends afterward. That would have to be enough. Because she had no doubt that all this passion would fade when they finally got back to the real world.

WHAT BEGAN IN the bathtub ended in a tangle of expensive Egyptian-cotton towels on the bathroom floor. He brought her to the edge again and again and she begged him to finish the job, even though she didn't want it to end. Greta knew that this might be the last experience they shared. She wanted every move, every sensation to be burned into her memory.

She'd never invite another man to her bed without thinking of Alex and what he had done to her body. Alex pulled her leg up along his hip and slowed his pace. God, he was the most beautiful man she'd ever touched. Why hadn't she realized this sooner?

Something had shifted between them, as if they'd both experienced a seismic sexual awakening. It hadn't happened four years ago, so why was it happening now? What had changed between them?

Her orgasm took them both by surprise. One moment she was whispering his name, her breath soft against his neck and then she was crying out in pleasure, her body spasming beneath his. He was caught unprepared and his reaction was almost primal. With a low groan he drove into her once more and then lost himself in the sweet sensations.

When he was finally completely spent, he pulled Greta into the curve of his body, hugging her to his side. "This is a nice way to begin the day," he said.

"I usually start with a bowl of oatmeal," Greta said with a laugh.

"Really?" He considered the fact for a moment and grinned. "I like that. Something I didn't know about you." He paused. "But are you saying my performance ranks right up there with oatmeal?"

"No! But if this was the way I started every day, I'd never get to work."

"What if it was?" Alex asked. "Haven't you ever thought about it? You and me, together? Every morning?"

"No," Greta lied. In truth, she had, but she'd been smart enough to push all those thoughts to the back of her mind. It was a matter of survival for her. Falling for Alex wasn't a possibility because she'd believed he wasn't interested in her romantically. But now, all that had changed. He'd admitted that there was something between them, something more than friendship.

Was he in love with her? Perhaps *lust* was a more appropriate word, she mused. Greta knew him well enough to read the signs. After meeting a girl, there was always a period of intense infatuation for him, when any woman, no matter her faults, seemed like the perfect mate. But as time went on, the thrill waned and he moved on. For her own well-being, Greta needed to be prepared for the worst. "You hate oatmeal."

"That's not the point," he said. "What I'm saying is, I'd like to think about us having breakfast. Not just today. But maybe tomorrow. And next week. And next year."

Greta scrambled to her feet and picked a towel off the edge of the tub to wrap around her naked body. She stepped to the mirror and ran her fingers through her wet hair. "You always think that way when you first meet a woman," she said. "But that doesn't mean it will last."

"I haven't just met you. And don't go comparing yourself to the other women in my life. You're different."

"We're both attractive adults with healthy sex drives. And we're both single and looking. But that doesn't mean anything. It's just…hormones."

Alex sat up and pulled a towel onto his lap, watching her as she moved around the bathroom. His brow was wrinkled with worry and she could see him trying to read her mood. Maybe she shouldn't be so pessimistic, but it was hard to be anything else when she was dealing with a guy who went through women like socks.

He joined her at the mirror, the towel wrapped at his hips. Slipping his arms around her waist, he rested his chin on her shoulder. "So what do you want to do?"

"I think we should get dressed and go in to town for breakfast. And then we should go back to Denver."

"That's not what I was talking about. I was talking about us."

"There isn't an us," she said.

"I think there might be," he said. "And I don't want to go back home. We have the cabin for the weekend. I think we should stay. The wicked witch is gone so why not take advantage of our good fortune?"

She turned around to face him, staring up into his oh-so-familiar eyes. She wanted to kiss him, to soothe all her doubts and insecurities. It would be so easy to believe him, to play along with the fantasy. But the risk was all hers to take. "I'm not going skiing," she said.

"Then, I'm not going skiing either," he said.

"Isn't that why you came here?"

"My plans have changed," he said. "I want to spend the day with you. What do you want to do?"

"I guess we could go into town and walk around. Maybe do some shopping." Shopping was Alex's least favorite pastime. "I guess I wouldn't mind skiing, if you'd ski with me."

"All right," he said, his expression brightening. He gave her a quick kiss. "Let's get dressed. We'll have some breakfast, hit the slopes and then have an early dinner in town. And we'll fit some shopping in there, too."

He walked out of the bathroom, leaving Greta to her own thoughts. The less time they spent shut up in this cabin, the better. There was only one activity available to them here, and though she could imagine a week in bed with him, she wasn't sure it was the best thing for her body or her heart. In the outside world, she'd have a chance to put this tangle of feelings into perspective.

Greta could see him getting dressed in the reflection of the mirror. Her gaze followed his movements. Muscles rippled on his back and her eyes dropped to his backside. He was an incredibly sexy man, from the top of his head to the tips of his toes.

What would it be like to have a man like Alex in her bed permanently, to wake up with him every morning and to fall asleep with him each night?

"Hurry up in there," he called, turning to face her. "We're burning daylight. And you don't have to spend an hour fixing your hair. It will just get messed up anyway."

She shook herself out of her idle contemplation. This was the real Alex Hansen. Impatient, focused, self-absorbed. Since he loved skiing, he was sure she'd love it too. "What should I wear?"

"You can wear my ski pants," he said. "Since we'll be skiing on the beginner runs, I can ski in jeans."

She walked into the room and he held out the pants. "I don't think those will fit," she said, examining them more closely.

"They might be a little baggy, but they'll keep you warm and dry."

She smiled to herself as she got dressed. How sweet of him to think that they'd be too big for her. She was worried they weren't made for a woman with curves. To her surprise, they fit just fine.

"You'll need warm socks," he said. He grabbed a pair from his duffel, then sat her down on the edge of the bed and grabbed her foot.

"I can dress myself," she murmured.

"I know you can. But it's more fun if I do it." He picked up her foot and pressed his lips to her instep. "I always thought you had pretty feet. Some women have kind of gnarly toes, but yours are really sexy."

"Oh, please. If the only sexy part of my body is my feet, it's a wonder you're attracted to me at all."

"I didn't say that," Alex replied as he slipped the wool sock over her toes. "If you recall, I haven't seen a whole lot of the rest of your body. I've been left to imagine what's under the clothes."

"You saw my body that night we spent in bed four years ago."

"I remember as much about that night as you do," he said. "I'd worried that it would probably ruin our friendship, but then it didn't."

"It was a silly thing to do," she said. "We could have wrecked everything."

"And what about now?"

"We're different people. Older and wiser."

He stared down at her foot, gently massaging her arch through the thick wool of the sock. "You're right. We are different." Alex smiled as he looked up at her and for the first time in their friendship, she didn't know what he was thinking. Greta searched his face for a clue to why he was smiling. Had things begun to change already?

He stood up, then bent closer and kissed her, a long, sweet, gentle kiss that seemed to go on forever. Any concerns she had were instantly wiped away. For the moment, she could believe that the affection between them was enough to weather any storm, even a sexual tsunami.

ALEX HAD ALWAYS loved spring skiing. The weather was warmer, the slopes sunny, and though the snow wasn't the best, he knew the season would be over soon, so his enjoyment was doubled.

He stood crossways on the run, Greta above him,

her poles planted in front of her in an attempt to stop herself from sliding down the hill. "You can do it," he called. "Big, wide, easy turns. Just like I taught you."

"It's too steep," she said, glancing around at the skiers gliding past her.

"It isn't if you just crisscross the run. You're not going to go straight down the mountain."

He'd expected the morning to be a long series of arguments, but to his surprise, Greta was trying her best to learn. In the past, she'd always just brushed off his offers to teach her to ski, but for some reason, she was putting a decent effort into this lesson.

Wincing, she shifted her skis downhill and began to move, sliding across the run on the packed snow. As she reached the edge, she put her ski tips together and made a beautiful turn, then headed back toward him, a wide smile on her pretty face.

"Keep going," he urged as she skied past him. She made another turn and when she passed again, he followed her, calling out encouragement as she gingerly made her way down the run.

"Now, try to get your skis back together again as soon as you've turned."

She screamed a couple times as she made a few dicey turns, but they reached the bottom of the hill without any falls. Alex skied up beside her and laughed. "See. I told you you could do it."

Greta clapped her mittened hands. But in her jubilation, she lost her balance and tipped to the side. Arms flailing, she fell into the snow, her skis sliding out from beneath her. She looked up at Alex, wide-eyed.

He chuckled, shaking his head. "Well, you'll get more comfortable as time goes on." He held out his hand to help her up, but instead, she pulled him down with her.

"Stop laughing at me," she said, throwing a damp mitten at his face.

"I'm not laughing at you," he protested. "I'm just enjoying the moment."

"The moment I humiliate myself in front of you?"

"No," he murmured, slipping his hand around her nape. He pulled her into a kiss, made all the more difficult by the tangle of skis and poles he had to work with. She responded reluctantly at first, but then sighed softly as she opened beneath his gentle assault. When he pulled back, Alex brushed a windblown lock of hair from her eyes. "I'm enjoying this moment."

Greta sent him a winsome smile. "This was fun," she said.

"Enough to make you want to try it again?"

"I think I've had enough humiliation for today. But maybe another time."

Alex helped her to her feet, then released her bindings with his pole. "What humiliation? You did really well."

"I fell at least thirty times. Maybe more."

"Oh, stop," Alex said, reaching down to grab her elbow. "It's not like all your clothes suddenly came off in the middle of the town square. This is a ski hill. People fall."

"But I seemed to do nothing but fall," she protested. "If you were trying to teach me to lie down in the snow, I'd be an expert." She struggled to pick up her skis, holding them in front of her at an awkward angle. "I know you'd rather be racing down some black diamond run instead of hanging out with me. Why don't I go warm up in the lodge and you can enjoy yourself a little."

"I like hanging out with you, Adler. You amuse me." He hooked his thumb under her chin and dropped a kiss on her lips. "I think we've had enough for today. Let's get some lunch. And after that, we can do a little shopping."

"Shopping? We're going to shop when there's skiing to be done?" Greta reached out and gently slapped the side of his head. "Are you all right?"

"I'm fine. I'd just rather spend my day with you than all alone on the slopes. Is there anything wrong with that?"

"Yes," she said. "You're acting like a—" Greta stopped, then began to fuss with her ski poles. "Never mind," she murmured.

"No, what?" Alex asked. "I'm acting like a what?"

"A boyfriend," Greta replied, fixing him with an uneasy expression. "It's just a little…unnerving."

Alex took her skis from her, balancing both pairs on his shoulder. "Maybe we ought to give that a try," he said.

"Give what a try?" Greta asked.

He glanced over at her. "Are you really that obtuse or are you—"

"I'm not obtuse."

"Then you're obviously trying to irritate me by playing dumb. I'm telling you that I think we should try dating. No, not dating. We should…be together."

"You're crazy," Greta said. "We can barely get along for two hours in a row. You expect us to survive a real relationship."

"We got along pretty well last night. And this morning. If you recall, we barely argued at all, which must be some kind of record for the two of us. And I'm thinking this afternoon will be even better." He grinned. "Practice does make perfect."

"This isn't skiing," she said. "You just can't decide to have a relationship and expect everything to work out. We're friends. We've always been friends. Besides, we can't have a relationship. We work together and at Johnson-Jacobs, there are rules against that sort of thing."

"What are you afraid of?" Alex asked.

"Nothing," Greta said. "Except the fact that you haven't managed a relationship longer than eight weeks in all the time I've known you. Why should I expect something between us to be any different?"

He shrugged. "I suppose you wouldn't. But do you really think I'd risk our friendship for some casual affair?"

They didn't speak as they returned Greta's rental

boots, skis and poles. She refused an offer of lunch and they headed back to the parking lot. He reached out and grabbed her hand, lacing his fingers through hers.

Greta glanced over at him. "It's what boyfriends do," he explained. "They hold their girlfriend's hand."

"What else do they do?" she asked.

"Anything their girlfriends want?" he said with a grin. "What do you want? Anything at all. Just name it."

She studied him shrewdly, her forehead wrinkled into a frown. "I heard about an antiques store in town," she said. "We could check it out."

"That sounds like loads of fun," he said.

Greta laughed out loud. "You sound too enthusiastic to be believable."

"No," he said. "I think it will be fun. Maybe we'll find one of those pottery things you've been looking for."

"Roseville," she said. "It's Roseville pottery."

"Right," he said. "Roseville. I'll have to remember that if I'm going to be your boyfriend."

"Don't get too far ahead of yourself there, sparky," she muttered. "We haven't set foot inside a store yet."

They drove into Aspen and parked the car near the antiques store that Greta had spotted. But this time, Alex slipped his arm around her waist as they strolled down the sidewalk.

"Is this it?" he asked, pointing to a small shop.

Greta stared into the window. "Yeah."

"Roseville," he repeated to himself.

They walked inside. Unlike their previous shopping trips, Alex didn't wander off and entertain himself. He stayed at Greta's side as she examined a shelf of colorful pottery. After she'd picked up several pieces, she shrugged. "Nothing here I want," she murmured.

"There has to be something in this store you want," he said.

"It's too expensive," she whispered. "Overpriced."

"If you could have any one, which would you want?" he asked.

She pointed to a small blue vase. "This one. It's wisteria. They're pretty rare." She wandered off to a far corner of the shop and he motioned to the clerk.

"Wrap this up," he said softly, handing her the vase. "And throw in…" Alex searched the shelves for an inexpensive item, then picked up an old milk bottle. "This." He gave the clerk a credit card. "And don't let her see what you're doing."

Alex strolled over to Greta's side and watched as she picked through some lace-edged table linens. Though he thought they were pretty, he wasn't quite sure what Greta would do with them. "Nice," he murmured.

After they'd browsed for another ten minutes, the clerk called him over. He signed the credit-card receipt and picked up his bag.

"What did you buy?" Greta asked as they walked out the front door.

He pulled the bottle from the bag. "An old milk bottle. I need something to put my quarters in for the Laundromat."

"Nice," she said, eyeing his purchase with approval.

Alex slipped his arm around her waist. "All this shopping has made me hungry. Should we eat out or head back to the cabin?"

She thought about his question for a moment, then shrugged. "Cabin," she murmured.

Though Alex knew the refrigerator was well stocked, he was hoping there was something back at the cabin that she wanted more than leftover Thai noodles.

5

THEY ATE DINNER in front of a roaring fire, the cartons of takeout spread in front of them like a feast. Greta was amazed at how easy things were between them, easier than they'd ever been. They'd always bickered like an old married couple, but now, Alex didn't seem to be interested in provoking her.

She thought back to grade school, to the first boy who'd ever taken an interest in her. He'd teased her mercilessly, chasing her around the playground, throwing stones at her or pulling her hair. Her mother had assured her that boys acted this way when they liked a girl.

Was that how it had been with Alex? Had he been so afraid of his feelings that he'd felt the need to keep her at arm's length? She wanted to believe that his newfound attraction to her was based on something more than just physical need.

"I had a good time today," she murmured, toying with the stem of her wineglass. "It was kind of strange."

"How?"

"I don't know. It was like we were ourselves, but different. We acted like…grown-ups."

"We are grown-ups," he said. Alex reached out and grabbed her hand, then placed a kiss in the center of her palm. A shiver skittered down her spine as her mind flashed an image of Alex, naked and aroused. She knew what he was thinking and she'd been unable to focus on anything else since the moment they walked in the front door.

They had the whole night in front of them, an empty cabin, a huge bed, everything they could possibly need. How could she possibly resist? "I like the new us," she said, smiling.

"Do you think the new us should try out that hot tub? I had a look at it earlier. It's filled and it's hot."

"It's also freezing outside," she said.

"You skied all afternoon," he said. "Certainly you're bold enough to brave a little snow on the deck. It's like that big bathtub upstairs. Only outside, beneath the stars."

Alex jumped to his feet and began to strip off his clothes. "Come on, Adler. I dare you."

Greta never backed down from one of Alex's dares and he knew it. She stood up and followed suit, until she wore nothing but her underwear. Alex was already naked as he picked up the wine and both glasses and headed for the door.

But when he stepped out into the snow, he howled.

"Move fast," he warned. "And if you want me to share the tub, you better take off the rest of your clothes."

She ran to the door and watched as he crossed the snow-covered deck. He set the wine and glasses down as he pulled the cover off the hot tub. Then he hopped into the steaming water, wincing until he was completely submerged. "Come on. You're going to get cold standing there."

Steeling herself, she ran across the deck, trying to follow his footsteps in the snow. When she reached the tub, she sat down on the side and swung her legs over into the water. Though the initial shock was painful, the allure of Alex, naked and wet, was enough to distract her. Greta sank beneath the surface and Alex met her in the middle.

"Naked," he murmured, pressing a kiss to the curve of her neck.

He reached behind her and unfastened her bra. Then, twisting his fingers in the waistband of her panties, he pulled them down along her legs. He draped both over the edge of the tub.

"Much, much better."

Greta wrapped her arms around his neck and kissed him, their bodies coming together beneath the bubbling water. He pulled her legs up against his hips as his hands slid over her slick skin. Was it any wonder she found this so easy? Seduction was a simple thing, given the right tools. A hot tub was an absolute necessity, as was a bathtub sized for two, French sheets, expensive wine and a cabin so remote that no one would disturb them. And, of course, a man she found end-lessly attractive.

He grasped her hips and pushed her up above the surface, then gently brought her back down, his erec-tion sliding against the crease between her legs. The sensation was incredibly powerful and Greta moaned softly.

"Like that?" he asked.

"Mmm," she replied, closing her eyes and tipping her head back.

He continued to move against her, pulling them both over to the edge of the tub where he could sit on an underwater ledge. Greta stretched out above him, her breasts brushing against his chest as his pace grew faster.

At first, she was aware of every stroke, every heart-beat, but as her need began to grow, her mind grew fuzzy and her limbs boneless. His lips were warm on her neck and he bit softly as he trailed kisses along her shoulder.

She wanted him inside her, only a condom wasn't anywhere at hand. Greta knew Alex always practiced safe sex and so had she. But for the first time in her life, she wanted to feel a man without any barriers between them. Birth control wasn't an issue since she took her pills faithfully.

She felt her need spiraling out of control and as the first spasm hit her, she slid down against him. Alex gasped as her body trembled. He pressed his lips to the spot between her breasts and held her close until the orgasm subsided.

When she grew still, Greta opened her eyes and stared down at him. "That was nice," he said.

"For me. Not for you. Yet."

"I can wait," he said. "I think sex in a hot tub is a bit overrated. But sex in a big bed after messing around in a hot tub…now, that's something I can get behind."

Greta pressed her forehead to his and slowly rocked against him. "So, should we get out of this tub and move to the bed?"

"Anybody home?"

The shout startled them both and Greta turned to see a man standing inside the brightly lit house. She slipped out of Alex's embrace and moved to the near edge of the tub. "Is that Dave?"

"Yeah," Alex said.

"What's he doing here?"

"I don't know. I guess he changed his mind."

"He can't find us together," she said, searching for an escape route. "Oh, God, our clothes are all over the floor."

"Get down," Alex said.

Greta sank beneath the water, pressing herself up against the edge. Alex pulled her back up. "You don't have to drown yourself," he said. Then, he leaned over the edge of the tub and called to Dave. "Out here."

"Don't call him out," Greta whispered.

"Hey! What are you doing here?" Alex asked.

"My sister had plans for tomorrow, so I thought I'd

drive up tonight and we could get in a day of skiing to-morrow," Dave said. "Is there someone else here?"

"Someone else? No. Why would you—"

"There's dinner for two in front of the fireplace," he said.

"Oh. Yeah. Greta came along when you decided to back out."

"Adler?"

"Yeah." Alex's hand drifted down Greta's body, coming to rest on her thigh. "I think she's probably upstairs reading. She said she wanted to turn in early. Exhausted from shopping, I guess. I'm just enjoying the hot tub."

"It's all right I came?" Dave asked.

"Sure. You know Adler. She's like one of the guys."

"Well, let me grab my stuff from the car and I'll join you. I hope there's beer."

"Sure," Alex said. "Lots of beer."

"I'll be right back."

A few seconds later, Alex pulled her out of the water. "Go. Quick. Run upstairs and get dressed. Then move my stuff to one of the other bedrooms."

Greta grabbed her underwear from the side of the tub and hurried back inside, steam wafting off her naked skin. She grabbed up her clothes, praying that Dave wouldn't walk through the door before she was safely upstairs.

Alex grabbed his jeans and tugged them on, then locked the door until she reached the upper landing.

"Get dressed and come back down," he called.

Breathless, Greta closed the bedroom door behind her and leaned back against it, her heart slamming in her chest. Though they'd pretended to be in a relationship for Thea Michaels, that behavior was easy enough to explain at the office. But a naked romp in a hot tub would have been far more complicated.

She raked her hands through her wet hair and glanced around the room, strewn with both of their belongings. So much for one last romantic night together. They'd be sleeping in separate beds tonight and the thought of being alone, with Alex in the next room brought an unexpected pang of sadness.

This wasn't good, she mused. In just one day, she'd become so infatuated that she couldn't imagine spending a night without him. Greta shook her head. "Get a grip," she muttered. "Fairy tales always come to an end."

ALEX SUFFERED THROUGH three beers and endless conversations about business, skiing and the size of Thea Michaels's advertising budget before he was able to break away. His mind had been on Greta from the moment she'd raced up the stairs, naked and wet and still flushed from the aftereffects of his seduction.

"You know what, I'm exhausted," Alex murmured, setting his beer bottle down on the coffee table. "I think I'm going to turn in."

"It's barely ten," Dave said.

"I know. But if we're going to ski tomorrow, we'll need to get up early."

"Is Adler going to ski with us?"

"No. She's just a beginner. I skied with her today, but she won't be able to keep up. Not that she'd want to."

Dave studied him shrewdly. "Is there anything going on between you two?"

"Why would you say that? We're friends."

"I don't believe a guy and a girl can be friends."

"Believe it," Alex said. "We've been friends for seven years."

"She is kind of pretty," Dave commented with a shrug.

Kind of pretty? "She's beautiful," Alex said.

"See, that's my point. If you think she's beautiful, then there has to be some attraction. Unless, of course, she's a total nightmare. One of those high-maintenance chicks who enjoys making guys squirm."

"No. She's nice."

"Then why haven't you slept with her?" Dave asked.

Alex shook his head. "We're not going to have this conversation. Greta and I are friends. Let's leave it at that."

"Have you slept with her?" Dave asked.

"No." It was a lie, but damned if he was going to spill his guts to Dave MacDonald. What had happened between him and Greta was private…intimate…and none of anyone's business. "I don't want to wreck our friendship."

Dave drew in a deep breath. "I don't get it. If I were here, alone, with a woman who looked like her, I'd at least give it a shot."

Though Alex had been waiting for Greta to come back down and join the party, he was glad she hadn't. He'd never thought much about how the other guys at work looked at Greta. And since dating between co-workers was off-limits, he'd never had to worry. But talk like this wasn't something he enjoyed.

It was clear that Dave sensed something might be going on. Maybe it was a good thing Greta hadn't come down. Would Dave be able to see the desire in his eyes? Would he be able to be in the same room with her without staring at her beautiful face and wanting to touch her?

"How many times have we partied until dawn and then skied the next day. Come on, man, you're not that old."

"I'm old enough," Alex said. He was old enough—to know that life wasn't an endless party. That strangers wouldn't be there when you really needed someone. And that finding a woman to spend a lifetime with was much more difficult than finding a woman to share his bed for a night.

"Well, I'm going to hit the hot tub before I turn in," Dave said.

"I'll see you in the morning." Alex picked up the mess from the coffee table and took it to the kitchen, then grabbed a few things from the refrigerator before heading upstairs. When he got to the door of the room he'd shared with Greta, he looked inside. The room and the bed were empty. He moved along to the next room and found Greta curled up reading a book.

"Hey," he murmured, closing the door behind him.

"Hey." She sat up and brushed her tousled hair from her face. "What do you have there?"

"Dessert," he said. "We didn't get to that earlier."

She smiled. "Aren't you a sweet man. What did you bring me?"

"Leftover tiramisu, carrot cake and some kind of chocolate layer cake." He set the takeout containers on the bed in front of her.

"Forks?"

Alex cursed. "No, I forgot forks. Let me go down and get some."

"That's all right," she said. "We can use our fingers."

He growled softly. "I like that."

Giggling, Greta scooped a bit of tiramisu onto her finger and held it out to him. He grabbed her hand and took her finger into his mouth, his gaze fixed on hers.

"Good?" she inquired.

"Mmm-hmm." Alex licked her skin clean then picked up a slice of the chocolate cake and fed her a bit.

"Has Dave gone to bed?"

Alex shook his head. "He's in the hot tub. After that, I think he'll turn in for the night. Then you and I can get our night started."

"No! If he finds out we're messing around, it will cause all kinds of complications."

"He's not going to find out. I promise, I'll be very, very quiet."

Greta shook her head. "No. If we're going to continue this, we'll do it back in Denver, where no one will notice. Not here. It's too risky."

"I'm not sure I'm going to like sneaking around. What if I want to kiss you at work? Maybe we should find a place to meet."

She sighed softly, shaking her head. "Do you want to lose your job over this?"

"No. The reason that rule was passed was because of an extramarital affair, not a relationship between two single people. We do good work. They're not going to fire us, Greta."

"How do you know? I need that job. I'm not going to spend another seven years at an agency trying to work my way up to senior art director. I'm almost there now."

Though Alex knew he could find a job at any agency in town, it was a bit different for creative types like Greta. "What do you propose we do then? I'll do whatever you want."

"We keep it a secret until we figure out what *it* actually is," Greta said.

"I already know what it is. It's a relationship."

"I think it's closer to a weekend fling right now."

He leaned closer and dropped a kiss on her lips. "Whatever it is, I'm liking it. A lot."

"Me, too," she said.

"I'm going to come back later," he said. "I'll leave before dawn. Dave won't suspect a thing." He wasn't going to mention that Dave already suspected something.

"Please don't," she said.

"We're not going to see each other tomorrow. He wants to ski and I couldn't think of a decent excuse not to."

"If you're going to ski, then I think I'm going to take your car and drive back to Denver. You can ride back with Dave."

"What if I made up some excuse so we could spend the day together?"

Greta reached out and smoothed her palm across his cheek. "I'm not going anywhere. It's not like this will be the only opportunity for us to be together." She frowned. "We do spend a lot of time together anyway."

"Not like this," Alex said. A fear had been nagging at him all day and he wanted to voice it, anxious for her reaction. "What if it isn't the same once we leave here? What if you want to go back to the way things were before? Like you did four years ago?"

"You're the one who wanted to do that," she said.

"That's not the way I remember it." Alex sighed. "I don't want to argue. I want to take off all our clothes, crawl beneath the covers and make love to you. Right now."

He saw the conflict etched across her features. In truth, she did have a lot more to lose than he did. No one was going to fire him from the agency. He handled two of their biggest clients. But Alex had to believe that a relationship between the two of them would barely cause any notice at all.

"Okay, I'll go," he said, sliding off the bed. "But leave your door unlocked. I might be back." He bent over the edge of the bed and touched his lips to hers. It began as a simple kiss, but the need between them was raw and immediate.

When he could finally pull himself away, Alex smiled. "Good night, Adler."

"Night, Hansen," she said with a winsome smile. "Sleep tight."

THE CABIN WAS SILENT and dark when Greta slipped out of her bedroom. A shiver skittered across her body in anticipation and she held her breath as she tiptoed from her room to Alex's. Wincing, she opened the door, then slipped inside.

He was lying in the center of the bed, the sheets twisted around his legs, his gorgeous body illuminated by the light filtering from the bathroom.

He sensed her presence before she even touched him. "I knew you'd come," he said as she crawled into bed beside him. She took in his handsome profile in the soft light, a smile curling the corners of his lips.

Alex wrapped his arms around her waist and pulled her body against his. "I like having you in my bed," he whispered. "What took you so long?"

"I wasn't sure I should come," she said.

"If you want, we can just cuddle."

"Cuddle?" she asked. Greta giggled. "I can't imagine that you're the type of man who likes to cuddle."

"I used to think that guys who liked to cuddle were wimps. But, I have to say, I enjoy a cuddle with you. Touching you and listening to you talk. Smelling your hair. Your hair smells really nice, by the way. Did anyone ever tell you that? I don't know why I didn't notice before."

"Where is Alex Hansen?" Greta asked with a laugh. "What have you done with the man I've always known?"

He pulled her closer, softly growling in her ear before he kissed her. "He's still here." The kiss deepened and Alex pulled her hips to his. He was already growing hard.

He was still wearing a T-shirt and sweatpants, but that didn't stop Greta. Her hands slid up beneath the T-shirt to smooth across his warm chest. "I never expected this," she murmured.

"Us. Together. Naked?" He chuckled softly. "Wait, we're clearly not naked." Alex got up on his knees and pulled his T-shirt over his head, tossing it onto the end of the bed. His sweatpants followed. "Better?"

Greta reached out and ran her fingers down his belly. "Much better."

"What about you?"

She wriggled out of the oversize T-shirt she wore and tossed it aside. "Now that we're both naked, let the cuddling commence."

He cupped her breast with his hand, teasing her nipple. His lips soon found the taut peak and Greta moaned softly as a wonderful wave of sensation coursed through her body. Already, she was starting to crave these feelings.

Everything about Alex made the intimate moments

so much more intense. She'd made love with other men, but there had never been such a magnetic pull between them. She couldn't resist Alex no matter how hard she tried. He was everything she'd ever wanted in a man. Why had it taken so long for her to recognize that?

Greta slipped her fingers through his hair, holding him close. He trailed a line of kisses to her other breast, then moved down to her stomach.

"You're so beautiful," he murmured, his lips soft on her skin.

She'd never really thought of herself in that way. But Alex had never lied to her. He truly believed the words he said and the notion that he found her physically pleasing made her feel powerful.

The seduction was slow and deliberate, each of them teasing and tempting until they were both overwhelmed with need. And when he pulled her beneath him and slipped between her legs, she was ready for the feel of him moving inside her.

She held her breath as he probed at her damp entrance and then slowly filled her. Greta shifted beneath him and he sucked in a sharp breath.

"Don't move," he murmured.

"But I want to move."

He groaned. "Why is this so different with you?" he asked. "I feel like a high school kid with you. Like I don't know what the hell I'm doing."

"I think you're doing a fine job," she said. "Word around the office is that you are pretty good at this."

"They talk about me? Who talks about me?"

"All the women. But I think it's idle speculation. You haven't slept with any of them," Greta said. "Have you?"

"No, Greta, the only coworker I've slept with is you. Oh, and Dave when we went camping up at Estes Park. We shared a tent."

"Can I move now?"

He drew a deep breath and shook his head. "No."

"Yes," she murmured.

"No," he repeated.

Greta arched against him, driving him a bit deeper. With a low growl, he grabbed her hips and rolled her on top of him. Greta stared down at him, her hair tangled around her face.

"Now you can move," he murmured, watching her through half-hooded eyes.

At first, she set a slow, lazy rhythm, watching his pleasure reflected in his gaze. But when he reached for her and pulled her down into a long kiss, Greta lost her focus for a moment, and surrendered to the warmth of his mouth.

They were so good together. After just one night, she realized no one else in the world could please her as much. As he drew her closer to her release, she couldn't deny her feelings any longer. She was in love with Alex. And she had been for a very long time, maybe even from the very start.

It had taken all her strength to deny it for so many years, but now, the stress seemed to dissolve in a single moment and she was free—free to believe that they had a future.

When he reached between them and touched her, she felt the first surge of an orgasm and before she could take another break, she was there, tumbling over the edge. She pressed her lips to his neck to keep from crying out. This was what she'd waited for, what she'd always hoped she'd find. And finding it with her best friend made it all the more wonderful.

When he came a minute later, silently, she held his face between her hands and whispered his name as his body shuddered beneath hers. This man had made a place for himself in her life, but now, he'd also found a place in her heart. What was she going to do with that? Greta wondered.

"If I'd ever known it would be this good, we would have made love much sooner," he said.

"We did make love," Greta reminded him.

"I know. But I don't think either of us was ready for it back then. Obviously we weren't, because we didn't recognize what we had."

"And now?"

"Now?" He paused, his gaze searching hers. "Now, I'm not sure I can do without this. I want you in my life, Greta."

"I am," she replied.

"Like this. Together. You and me."

"It's been one weekend," she said.

"It's been seven years," he reminded her.

Greta snuggled against him. He was right. They

knew each other better than most married couples did. "I've only really liked you for five of them," she said.

"What?" He frowned. "You didn't like me when you met me?"

"No, not at all. I thought you were full of yourself. And you just charmed everyone in the room. Every girl in the office thought they might get lucky with you and you didn't do a thing to discourage them. I thought you were dangerous."

"Dangerous? I am a ninja when it comes to advertising."

Greta remembered that day so clearly. She'd decided then and there that she'd lock up her heart when Alex was around, just for her own safety. Maybe that's why their friendship had worked, because she'd never given in. Would her surrender now be the beginning or the end of what they were?

"So are you going to sleep in our bed, Adler? Or are you going to shuffle off to your own lonely room?"

"I can stay until three," she said.

"Four," he countered.

"Three-thirty." She kissed him. "Set the alarm on your cell phone."

"Why?" he murmured. "We won't be doing any sleeping."

6

ALEX STRODE FROM the elevator to the wide office doors of Johnson-Jacobs Advertising, anxious to see Greta for the first time since their weekend together.

Yesterday, she'd left with his car, driving back to Denver on her own. He'd found the keys on the kitchen counter of his apartment when he'd returned, along with a note letting him know that she'd speak to him at the office.

He'd spent the whole night tossing and turning, wondering why she wasn't sharing his bed again that night. Had she changed her mind about embarking on a romantic relationship? Would they go another four years before they enjoyed another intimate encounter?

He knew Greta well enough to know that she was nothing if not practical, a characteristic that tempered his own impulsiveness. That's why they made such a good team, he mused.

He pushed open the doors and their receptionist, Emily, smiled at him. "Red alert. Rich was looking for you. And he doesn't look happy. Oh, and Thea Michaels is waiting in your office. I sent out for her nonfat, double-foam, half-caf latte and she seems content for now with my copy of *Vogue*."

"Did Rich say what he wanted?"

"No. But rumor has it that the diva was waiting for him when he got in this morning. After they talked, his mood had changed."

A sick feeling washed over Alex. "Have you seen Greta?"

"No. I'm not sure she's in yet. Do you want me to check?"

Alex drew in a deep breath to steady himself. "I'll just check, myself." He strode toward the art department. When he reached Greta's office, he laid his briefcase on her desk and opened it. He withdrew the pretty blue vase he'd bought her, along with a small bouquet of tea roses. It was a beautiful piece, he thought to himself. And all the better because he knew Greta would love it.

Unfortunately, he doubted he'd be there to see her reaction. He was needed in the boss's office. Though he'd just enjoyed the most wonderful, incredible, passionate weekend of his life, the realities of his professional life were enough to dull the shiny memories. He'd also have to deal with Thea. And, if his suspicions were correct, he and Greta were going to have to pay for their delightful interlude at Thea's mountain retreat.

He drew a ragged breath and tried to work up a decent case of remorse. But the truth was, he didn't regret a single moment of his weekend with Greta. "I guess I better go see what he wants."

Alex started down the hall to his boss's office, going over a litany of possibilities in his mind. But there was only one that stood out.

The strict fraternization code was about to be applied. Rich's assistant was awaiting his arrival and with a worried look, ushered him into the office. To Alex's surprise, Greta was sitting on the sofa, her legs crossed primly in front of her. And to his relief, Thea had left. His gaze met Greta's and he grinned at her. "Morning, Adler," he said.

She smiled weakly. "Good—good morning," Greta murmured, staring at her hands. She looked up at Richard Johnson. "Let's just get on with this, shall we?"

"Have a seat, Alex." He indicated a chair and Alex quickly sat down. "I'll get right to the point. I understand that you two are involved romantically. Since you're aware of agency policy, my question is, what are we going to do about this?"

Greta shook her head. "Sir, I think I should first say that Alex and I are—"

"What are our options?" Alex interrupted.

"We're not involved," Greta explained.

"Yes, we are," Alex countered.

"No!" Greta cried. "It was just a—a one-night thing. It's over. Completely over. And it will never, ever happen again."

"No, it's not over," Alex said. "At least not as far as

I'm concerned. And it was two nights." He held up two fingers. "Two."

"Well, which is it?" Johnson asked impatiently.

"What are you doing?" Greta asked Alex. "Don't joke about this."

"I'm not joking," Alex assured her. "Even now, after an entire weekend spent in bed, all I can think about is getting you home." He gave Johnson a shrug. "Sorry, but it's the truth."

"Hmm," Johnson said. "That's a problem."

Greta jumped to her feet and crossed the room to stand in front of him. "What are you doing?" she said under her breath. "We're going to lose our jobs."

"I was about to promote you," Johnson said to Greta. "Senior art director for the Sunrise Airlines account."

"We got the account?" Greta asked.

Johnson nodded. "They called this morning to give me the news. They were very impressed with your print campaign."

Greta turned to Alex, sending him a pleading look. "I've worked for seven years to get to this position."

"I know," Alex said. "And you deserve this promotion more than anyone I know." He turned to Johnson. "So, Rich, if I agree to leave, then there is no fraternization and we're cool, right? Greta can keep her job."

"You run one of our largest accounts," Rich said. "I don't think we want to lose—"

"Yes or no?" Alex asked.

"No!" Greta said. "This is ridiculous. Neither one of us has to give up our job. We'll just agree that it's over."

"But it's not," Alex said. "I think—no, I'm pretty sure that I'm in love with you. Very sure. And I want to spend as much time as possible with you. Besides, I can get a job anywhere."

"Hold on there," Rich said. "What are we talking about? I can't afford to lose you. If you go, Alex, Thea Michaels will follow. And I need you, Greta, on Sunrise Airlines."

Alex pushed to his feet. "Then, Rich, I think you've got a bigger problem than I can solve for you. If you fire Greta, then I go. Maybe you ought to just fire us both and get it over with."

"What?" Greta asked. "No! That would be a bad idea. I—I'll go."

"I don't know…" Rich said.

Alex shook his head. "Nope. She goes, I go." He slipped his arms around Greta's waist and pulled her close, then kissed her softly. "You look wonderful," he whispered. "I missed you last night."

"I missed you, too," she said.

"I love you, Adler."

She smiled, then smoothed her hand over the chest of his starched shirt. "I love you, too, Hansen."

Alex kissed her again, lingering over her lips before he finally stepped back. "Well, I'm sure you will figure this all out, Rich. Whatever you decide, just let me know. I've got to track down Thea Michaels and make sure she's not upset with me, too."

"I told her to wait in your office," Johnson said. "You know, she's really a pain in the ass."

"Oh, my gosh, yes!" Greta cried. "You should spend a little time with her. She called me fat."

Johnson frowned. "She called you fat?"

Satisfied that all would be well, Alex walked out of the boss's office and headed to his own. As expected, Thea was waiting for him, casually flipping through a magazine as she sipped her morning coffee. "You're here early," he said.

She looked up and smiled, her gaze slowly drifting down his body and back to his face. "I had important business," she said.

"Did you tattle to my boss about this weekend?" He kept his tone light, hoping that a confession would give him exactly what he needed to turn this situation around.

"I might have mentioned your little tryst."

"Well, I guess I have you to thank you then. I'm sure they'll find you a new account manager who can handle these little games you enjoy so much."

Her expression froze. "What are you talking about?"

"I'm done here. I'm no longer—"

"No!" she cried. "He was supposed to fire her, not you."

"Well, I quit. So she could keep her job. I'm in love with her and I'm willing to do anything to protect her. So don't even think of going after her, Thea. You can toss me in your nasty little oven, but leave her alone."

Thea opened her mouth, then snapped it shut. She drew a deep breath, then sent him a grudging smile.

"All right. You win. I'm sorry. I was just having a little fun."

"I don't think messing with peoples' careers is considered fun. Listen, I love my job here at Johnson-Jacobs. I'm damn good at what I do, which I think I've proved to you quite well. But obviously, that's not good enough."

"He fired you?" Thea asked.

"No, I told you, I quit. Why don't you go back in? If you can straighten this out with Rich, I might forgive you."

She stood and crossed the office to stand in front of him. Then, Thea pushed up on her toes and kissed his cheek. "You're a good man," she murmured. "Has anyone ever told you that?"

"Yes," he said, recalling Greta's words to him. And for the first time in his life, he believed the words were true.

GRETA STOOD NERVOUSLY at her desk. Her meeting with Rich Johnson had been cut short the minute Alex had walked out of the office. She'd been ordered back to work without further comment.

She stared at the small vase that sat next to her computer, the lovely wisteria flowers cascading over the edges. Alex had filled the vase with white tea roses and the scent of them filled her office.

Greta stood up nervously. But she couldn't stay at her desk. She needed to find Alex and talk to him. This was ridiculous! He'd put in years of hard work to get where he wanted to be and now he was willing to throw it all away just because they spent a weekend in bed? There was no way she'd allow him to do that.

She strode out to the lobby and looked at the receptionist. "How long ago did Thea leave?"

"A couple of hours," Emily said. "And then Alex left and Rich caught up to him at the elevators and they went downstairs together. What happened?"

"Nothing," Greta said.

"Is this about you and Alex?"

"You know?"

"Everyone knows," she said.

"How did it get around so fast?" Greta asked.

"What?"

Greta frowned. "What are you talking about?"

"The thing you have with Alex. Your friendship. Everyone can tell it's more than that. We've all been wondering when you were finally going to admit it to yourselves. It's blatantly obvious that you two are in love with each other."

"We are?"

Emily laughed, shaking her head. "The way you flirt and fight and then flirt all over again. All of us girls have been waiting for the wall to finally come down."

"Well, it came down, all right," Greta said. "And now, Alex plans to quit so I can keep my job. I think we should go back to being friends, but he wants to continue what we started."

"You can't go back," Emily said. She leaned forward. "Is he as good in bed as we all imagine him to be?"

Greta pushed away from the receptionist's desk, wagging her finger. "I'll never tell."

"Speak of the devil, there he is," Emily said, her gaze fixed on the wide glass doors.

Greta turned around and watched as Alex walked across the atrium to the front doors of the agency. When he spotted her inside, he grinned. Greta felt a nervous flutter in her stomach. He looked so happy. How could he be happy if he just quit his job?

He pulled open the doors and strode up to her, dropping a kiss on her lips. "Hi. You're just the girl I've been looking for."

"Where have you been? I've been trying to call you."

"I had a lot of thinking to do."

"You can't quit," Greta said.

"I already did. And then Rich convinced me to stay."

"He's not going to fire you?"

Alex shook his head. "Nope. And he's not going to fire you either."

"But what about the policy?"

"Well, it seems that the policy only applies to two single people carrying on a relationship within this office."

Greta glanced around, noticing a small crowd gathering in the lobby. "What are you talking about?" she whispered.

"I'm talking about us. You and me. If we're not single, they can't fire either one of us."

"I—I don't understand. We are single."

"That can be remedied."

Greta watched as he slowly dropped to one knee. He took her hand in his and reached into his pocket. "We've known each other for seven years. And we've been best friends for most of that time. You've seen me through good times and bad and no matter what I've said or done, you've always stuck by me. You are the most important woman in my life and I want to keep it that way."

"Get up," she whispered, her gaze frantically scanning the room. The crowd moved in closer to hear what Alex was saying. "Everyone's watching."

"Good. Because I want everyone to know exactly how I feel about you." He turned to face their coworkers. "I love Greta Adler," he shouted. "And I'm pretty sure she loves me. Does anyone have a problem with that?"

"No!" the crowd shouted, the cry mixed with laughter and cheers.

He turned back to Greta. "Since we have their approval, then I'm going to proceed. Greta, I love you. I want to spend my life with you. Will you marry me?"

"Are you crazy?" she asked.

"Yeah. Crazy in love. What do you say? Let's not waste any more time. I want to be with you." He reached into his pocket and withdrew a velvet-covered box. "I'm not sure if you'll like this one. If you don't, the jeweler has others to choose from." He opened the box and a diamond ring twinkled in the lights from the lobby.

Greta held her breath as he took it out and held it at her fingertip.

"Say yes," Alex urged. "I promise I'll make you happy."

Her mind spun and her heart pounded. For a moment, she thought she might faint from the whirl of emotion inside her. Everything she saw in his eyes told her that his words were true. She'd imagined the day he'd finally fall in love for good, but she'd never dreamed that his love would be for her.

He was her best friend and now he was her lover. Was it such a stretch to think that he could be her husband as well? "Are you just doing this so we can keep our jobs?"

"No," he said. "I'm doing this because I can't imagine spending another day without you in my life. I think it's time we made it official."

"Say yes," Emily whispered.

The crowd around them agreed and they voiced their own pleas for an answer to his proposal. Greta didn't have to think about what to say. Alex was right. They'd been in love for a very long time. "I do love you," she said. "And—"

"And?"

"And I will marry you, Alex Hansen. My answer is yes."

Their coworkers burst into a round of cheers and Alex got to his feet. He slipped the ring on her finger, then pulled her into a long, deep kiss, his hands cupping her face gently. When he finally drew back, he smiled down at her. "I don't know what I would have done if you hadn't said yes," he murmured. "You're the one for me."

Greta pushed up on her toes and kissed him again. "I know. I'm glad you finally figured that out."

"What's going on here?"

Rich Johnson's booming voice filled the lobby and the crowd around them quickly dispersed. He frowned at Alex and Greta, then shook his head. "This is exactly what that fraternization policy is meant to prevent. Public displays of affection in my lobby. A client could walk in at any minute. What would—"

"She said yes," Alex interrupted.

"Well, then, I guess my problem is solved," Rich replied. "Now that it is, I think we need to meet about the Sunrise account. Adler, I hope you can work with your soon-to-be husband without too many problems."

"Of course," Greta said. Her husband. Alex was about to become her husband. Though the concept was a bit hard to believe, it certainly didn't scare her. She could envision a life with Alex, a future, a family, a home they shared.

"Actually, we're going to take the afternoon off," Alex said, lacing his fingers through hers. "We'll be back tomorrow morning, bright and early. We can meet then."

He pulled her along, opening the wide glass door in front of them. When they reached the elevator, Greta took a deep breath. "Are we really engaged?"

"Did you think that was all just for show?" Alex asked.

"No, I—"

The bell rang. When the elevator doors opened, he drew her inside. The moment they closed, Greta found herself wrapped in his embrace. His lips came down on hers in a very convincing kiss. "We are," she said with a satisfied smile.

"Yes, we are."

"Where are we going?"

"There's a little trail of bread crumbs that leads right to your bed. I think it would be best if we follow them."

"Will there be a witch waiting for us at the other end?"

"No," Alex said. "Just years of happy endings."

"I can live with that," Greta said. She smiled and kissed him again. This was all she'd ever wanted, this fairy tale, this handsome prince. She'd thought she'd come to the end of the tale, but now, it was beginning all over again. And they would live happily ever after.

* * * * *

PASSION

Harlequin® *Blaze*

COMING NEXT MONTH
AVAILABLE APRIL 24, 2012

#681 NOT JUST FRIENDS
The Wrong Bed
Kate Hoffmann

#682 COMING UP FOR AIR
Uniformly Hot!
Karen Foley

#683 NORTHERN FIRES
Alaskan Heat
Jennifer LaBrecque

#684 HER MAN ADVANTAGE
Double Overtime
Joanne Rock

#685 SIZZLE IN THE CITY
Flirting with Justice
Wendy Etherington

#686 BRINGING HOME A BACHELOR
All the Groom's Men
Karen Kendall

REQUEST YOUR FREE BOOKS!
2 FREE NOVELS PLUS 2 FREE GIFTS!

Harlequin *Blaze*

red-hot reads!

YES! Please send me 2 FREE Harlequin® Blaze™ novels and my 2 FREE gifts (gifts are worth about $10). After receiving them, if I don't wish to receive any more books, I can return the shipping statement marked "cancel." If I don't cancel, I will receive 6 brand-new novels every month and be billed just $4.49 per book in the U.S. or $4.96 per book in Canada. That's a saving of at least 14% off the cover price. It's quite a bargain. Shipping and handling is just 50¢ per book in the U.S. and 75¢ per book in Canada.* I understand that accepting the 2 free books and gifts places me under no obligation to buy anything. I can always return a shipment and cancel at any time. Even if I never buy another book, the two free books and gifts are mine to keep forever.

151/351 HDN FEQE

Name _____ (PLEASE PRINT)

Address _____ Apt. #

City _____ State/Prov. _____ Zip/Postal Code

Signature (if under 18, a parent or guardian must sign)

Mail to the **Reader Service**:
IN U.S.A.: P.O. Box 1867, Buffalo, NY 14240-1867
IN CANADA: P.O. Box 609, Fort Erie, Ontario L2A 5X3

Not valid for current subscribers to Harlequin Blaze books.

Want to try two free books from another line?
Call 1-800-873-8635 or visit www.ReaderService.com.

* Terms and prices subject to change without notice. Prices do not include applicable taxes. Sales tax applicable in N.Y. Canadian residents will be charged applicable taxes. Offer not valid in Quebec. This offer is limited to one order per household. All orders subject to credit approval. Credit or debit balances in a customer's account(s) may be offset by any other outstanding balance owed by or to the customer. Please allow 4 to 6 weeks for delivery. Offer available while quantities last.

Your Privacy—The Reader Service is committed to protecting your privacy. Our Privacy Policy is available online at www.ReaderService.com or upon request from the Reader Service.

We make a portion of our mailing list available to reputable third parties that offer products we believe may interest you. If you prefer that we not exchange your name with third parties, or if you wish to clarify or modify your communication preferences, please visit us at www.ReaderService.com/consumerschoice or write to us at Reader Service Preference Service, P.O. Box 9062, Buffalo, NY 14269. Include your complete name and address.

HB11B

Julia McKee and Adam Sutherland never got along in college, but somehow, several years after graduation, they got stuck sharing the same bed on a weekend getaway with mutual friends. Can this very wrong bed suddenly make everything right between them?

Read on for a sneak peek from
NOT JUST FRIENDS by Kate Hoffmann.

Available May 2012, only from Harlequin® Blaze™.

"DO YOU REMEMBER the day we met?" Julia asked.

Adam groaned. "Oh, God, don't remind me. It was not my finest moment. My mind and my mouth were temporarily disengaged. I'd hoped you'd find me charming, but somehow, I don't think that was the case." He took her hand and pressed a kiss to her wrist, staring up at her with a teasing glint in his eyes.

Julia's gaze fixed on the spot where his lips warmed her skin. "Does that usually work on women?" she asked. "A little kiss on the wrist? And then the puppy-dog eyes?"

His smile faded. "You think I'm just playing you?"

"I've considered it," Julia said. But now that she saw the hurt expression on his face, she realized she'd been wrong.

She drew a deep breath and smiled. "I'm starving. Are you hungry?" Julia hopped out of bed, then grabbed his hand and pulled him up. "I can make us something to eat."

They wandered out to the kitchen, her hand still clasped in his, and when they reached the refrigerator, she pulled the door open and peered inside.

Grabbing a carton of eggs, she turned to face him. His hands were braced on either side of her body, holding the door open. Julia felt a shiver skitter over her skin.

Slowly, Adam bent toward her, touching his lips to hers. Julia had been kissed by her fair share of men, but it had never felt like this. Maybe it was the refrigerator sending cold air across her back. Or maybe it was just all the years that had passed between them and all the chances they'd avoided because of one silly slight on the day they'd met.

He drew back, then ran his hand over her cheek and smiled. "I've wanted to do that for eight years," he said.

Julia swallowed hard. "Eight?"

He nodded. "Since the moment I met you, Jules."

*Find out what happens in NOT JUST FRIENDS
by Kate Hoffmann.*

Available May 2012, only from Harlequin® Blaze™.

HBEXP0412

Harlequin *Presents*®

Royalty has never been so scandalous!

THE
SANTINA
CROWN

When Crown Prince Alessandro of Santina proposes
to paparazzi favorite Allegra Jackson it promises
to be *the* social event of the decade!

Harlequin Presents® invites you to step into the decadent
playground of the world's rich and famous and rub shoulders
with royalty, sheikhs and glamorous socialites.

**Collect all 8 passionate tales written by *USA TODAY*
bestselling authors, beginning May 2012!**